IMMORTAL'S PENANCE

ALSO BY L.A. ALBER

As Lisa Alber

Kilmoon
Whispers in the Mist
Path into Darkness

IMMORTAL'S PENANCE

A LABYRINTH OF SOULS NOVEL

BY

L.A. ALBER

ShadowSpinners Press

Cover art by Josephe Vandel.
Book design by Matthew Lowes.

ShadowSpinners Press
shadowspinnerspress.com

Typeset in
Minion Pro by Robert Slimbach
and IM FELL Double Pica by Igino Marini.
The Fell Types are digitally reproduced
by Igino Marini, www.iginomarini.com.

Learn more about
the Labyrinth of Souls game at
matthewlowes.com/games.

With love to Arlene Joyce Alber, the benign goddess-mother of our family, rest in peace.

Author's Note

I had a blast writing this story, and I'd like to thank Matthew Lowes for creating the Labyrinth of Souls, a world ripe for storytelling, an underworld as diverse as our imaginations. *Immortal's Penance* is my first foray into writing fantasy, so I extend a huge "thank you" to ShadowSpinners publisher (and editor extraordinaire) Christina Lay for reading early pages and gently steering me in the right direction for this genre. What works for crime fiction/mystery (my usual genre) doesn't necessarily work for fantasy. Great learning lessons!

I'd also like to thank Elizabeth Engstrom, Cheryl Owen-Wilson, and Cynthia Ray for their invaluable feedback.

As initial inspiration for this story—that is, bog bodies!—I'm indebted to one of my favorite mystery writers, Erin Hart.

Although set on the Isle of Man, I elected to use Americanisms in most cases. For example, "sweater" instead of the British "jumper." However, in some cases I did use the Britishism, such as "torch" for flashlight. Also, this novel plays with and broadly interprets the world of Celtic myth for storytelling purposes. Anything goes in the Labyrinth of Souls.

Editor's Preface

Dungeon Solitaire: Labyrinth of Souls is a fantasy game for tarot cards, written by Matthew Lowes and Illustrated by Josephe Vandel. In the game you defeat monsters, disarm traps, open doors, and explore mazes as you delve the depths of a dangerous dungeon. Along the way you collect treasure and magic items, gain skills, and gather companions.

Now ShadowSpinners Press is publishing this and other stand-alone novels inspired by the game. Each *Labyrinth of Souls* novel features a journey into a unique vision of the underworld.

The Labyrinth of Souls is more than an ancient ruin filled with monsters, trapped treasure, and the lost tombs of bygone kings. It is a manifestation of a mythic underworld, existing at a crossroads between people and cultures, between time and space, between the physical world and the deepest reaches of the psyche. It is a dark mirror held up to human experience, in which you may find your dreams … or your doom. Entrances to this realm can appear in any time period, in any location. There are innumerable reasons why a person may enter, but it is a place antagonistic to those who do, a place where monsters dwell, with obstacles and illusions to waylay adventurers, and whose very walls can be a force of corruption. It is a haunted place, ever at the edge of sanity.

IMMORTAL'S PENANCE

CHAPTER ONE

Isle of Man, British Crown dependency, Irish Sea, October, 1954

Malone Wolfe's crew of two men ambled away, leaving him alone with his excavation foreman, Anghus Ward, a crusty old local who revealed his aversion to Malone in the set of his lips and restless clenching of his fists. Malone didn't give a shite about Anghus's attitude, only about the work itself. The old git had probably never stepped off the island—a tiny life too horrifying to imagine—and therefore didn't comprehend the significance of the artifact buried beneath layers of peat.

Malone decided to gift Anghus his paltry bit of authority for the day. "Fine. Let's close the site down until tomorrow."

He zipped up his leather jacket and shoved his hands into his blue jeans pockets. The chill had mounted over the last few weeks, and it wouldn't be long before winter forced him to suspend the dig for the year anyhow. Still, the men's insubordination chafed at him. Just gone three o'clock; they had nearly two hours worth of light left.

"They'll not be back until tomorrow afternoon, if that." Anghus's gaze slid toward Malone, gauging him, and then away again. "Festivities and all."

Malone spotted three bonfires from their viewpoint above the village and Peel Castle, a 14th century Viking fortification at water's edge. His nostrils twitched at the smell of smoke, and the usual tension wormed its way up his spine. Across the Irish Sea, an autumnal glow outlined the Mountains of Mourne in Northern Ireland and illuminated the castle in a rosy glow.

Unbelievable that the rigors of war and then post-war recovery hadn't left their mark on local life. The villagers went about their breakfast of barley pottage as if the new, young queen and a ration-free world that included butter, sugared sweets, and cheese didn't exist. In the cities, jazz clubs and beatniks thrived, but you'd never know that either.

Instead, the Manx people, natives of old Celtic stock, clung to their beliefs, including, as Malone had just learned, the idea of Samhain, the Gaelic Day of the Dead.

Anghus's gaze wandered over the trench that marred the hillside. A dark expression that Malone preferred not to examine flitted across his features. Without word, Anghus retreated down the hillside toward the village. The nervy bugger.

Malone settled the picks, shovels, brushes, and other implements of his trade in a neat pile beneath a lone hawthorn tree. Standing a scrawny five feet high, its clawed branches flapped in the breeze like skeleton limbs. Malone sat back on his haunches and for the hundredth time surveyed the hawthorn's location in relation to the ditch his team had dug in the peat bog. If his measurements were correct, they'd find the bog body's head below the hawthorn.

He said a prayer that the roots hadn't damaged the artifact and jotted a few notes about the work completed that day. He'd hoped to excavate past the ankles, but they had only reached the heels. Meticulous work, uncovering a bog body—and this one? He whistled to himself, an exclamation without words. The sound echoed around him and lifted into the air. Toward Peel Castle, a dog bayed in ghostly response, and from the other side of the hill bonfire revelers hushed for a moment before resuming their Day of the Dead revelries.

Malone lowered himself into the ditch and followed a path marked out with twine toward the bog body's feet. Uncovering history made his heart soar with possibility and mystery; it was an itch he often scratched in the dead of night when sleep eluded him. With trowels and brushes he scraped away peat like a sculptor revealing the figure within a slab of marble.

He pulled off one of his cracked horsehide work boots and held it up alongside the bottom of one of the exposed mummified feet. A tall man, Malone had a tough time finding size fourteen shoes. Yet his feet were childlike in size compared to the bog body's feet. Amazing. Perhaps this giant of an ancient man had been idolized as a deity.

He pulled on his boot while examining the foot. The unique chemical attributes within peat bogs preserved bodies the way pickling preserved fruit. This shriveled specimen was in perfect condition down to the hairs on the tops of its toes and the calluses on its heels. No doubt about it, this discovery would make Malone's reputation and land him on top of the clamoring pile of archaeologists in search of grants and academic accolades.

Knowing he shouldn't, he pressed the back of his index finger against one of the foot calluses. Smooth and lumpy at the same time. His finger twitched with the thrill of the find and the foot twitched along with it.

"What the hell?"

He jerked his hand away and chided himself for allowing his mind to play games with him. The lingering effects of battle fatigue left over from the war. Nothing more. The mummified foot was just that—mummified. Satisfied that he wasn't losing his war-torn wits, he set off in search of supper.

CHAPTER TWO

In the village, music echoed out of several pubs and houses. Anghus had mentioned the custom of setting dinner places for deceased loved ones and leaving food outside to pacify the other crowd through the long winter. By "other crowd," he meant all manner of fey creatures of Celtic lore. Malone wasn't sure what the bonfires represented in this archaic local tradition, but it didn't matter. It seemed the dead, not to mention the other crowd, must be respected.

Malone stood irresolute in the central square. Jovial sounds from the cottages and bonfires surrounded him. The lonely ping of a far-off memory startled him. He scowled and headed toward the closest pub, The Highwayman, to grab a pint and a bowl of seafood chowder before heading to his rental cottage. While the drunken revelries ensued, he'd use the extra hours to outline a paper he planned to write for the journals.

In the pub, local men in tweed caps and fisherman sweaters peered at Malone and returned to their various conversations. The pub man, Fergus, drew a Guinness.

Malone grabbed a stool and watched the foam on his pint settle before Fergus topped it off and handed it over. Malone ordered his chowder. Fergus nodded and proceeded down the bar, chatting with his regulars as he filled their pints.

The door opened to a blast of cold air and plaintive dog howls. Anghus took over the stool next to Malone. He'd never run into Anghus at this particular pub before. Maybe the old fella was thawing at long last.

"Ol' Moddey Dhoo is more restless than usual this year, eh?" Fergus said.

Anghus nodded. "To be expected."

Fergus glanced at Malone. "Ay, no surprise."

Malone kept his mouth shut and his eyes trained on a framed print hanging on the wall behind the bar that featured a toucan with a pint balanced on its beak and the slogan "Lovely day for a Guinness."

Anghus ordered a whiskey and inclined his head toward Malone. Fergus poured two shots.

"*Shoh Slaynt!*" Anghus cheered and knocked his glass against the counter top before drinking. Malone followed suit. What the hell. This was the first time the old man had deigned to socialize with him off the excavation site.

"Veil is extra thin this year," Anghus said.

"Ay." Fergus poured two more shots, ignoring Malone's "no more for me."

"On with you," Anghus said. "You'll not be getting any work done tomorrow anyhow."

"Sod you all," Malone said and tossed back his shot.

After three more shots, hard edges softened. The soup arrived and Malone ate fast to help soak up the alcohol. Beside him, Anghus's bushy eyebrows waggled when he blinked. He hunched like a gnome and periodically swiveled his head to observe Malone while talking with Fergus and the other men along the bar.

At Anghus's nod, Fergus poured a sixth round for each of them. Malone waved Fergus away, but Fergus poured anyhow. "*Shoh slaynt*," Anghus said again.

Malone lost track of events about then. At one point, Anghus grabbed his arm as he wobbled on his stool. The bottles on the shelves wavered and conversations sounded like word mush. The dog's hollowed-out cries continued to seep into the room whenever the door opened.

Yes, Malone had heard the tales about Moddey Dhoo, the Black Dog ghost of Peel Castle, the supposed site of King Arthur's lost Avalon. Malone recalled that the dog—sometimes called "Caval" after King Arthur's favorite hunting dog—was said to be a black spaniel with a curly coat. Much was said on this Isle of Man.

Bollocks, the lot of it.

The older gents along the bar nodded in response to something Malone had missed.

"What say you?" Anghus said.

Silence met the question.

"That question for me?" Malone said.

Anghus nodded. "Can you feel how thin the veil is?"

Malone remembered and dismissed the fleeting notion that the bog body's toe had twitched. "Can't say that I do. Haven't felt much since—" he stopped himself before saying *the war*. "I don't believe in a veil."

Fergus hissed. "Said like a true comeover."

Malone had heard that one before—a true outsider.

"Whether you believe or not," Anghus said, "the other crowd hovers close at hand."

"Moddey isn't hovering," one of the old codgers said. "That phantom dog's already here."

Malone snorted into his pint as he drank.

"The archaeologist scoffs at the Black Dog ghost of Peel Castle," Fergus announced. "No surprise there."

"I didn't say a word," Malone said. "I enjoy the stories as much as the next man."

Anghus set a knobby hand on the counter in a quiet movement that nevertheless communicated his strained relationship with Malone, the outsider who dared to dig up their history. He tapped his fingers in agitated fashion. "Stories, no. That would be the truth you're hearing."

"And what truth might that be?"

Anghus squinted at Malone with eyes like two brown shards of glass. "I'd be careful on a night like tonight. What with the veil thin, some people might imagine the bog body lives."

"Oh, piss off."

"Ay, and with the bonfires and drinking. Wouldn't do to have people wandering too close to your precious site. Never know what devil will get inside a person."

Shite. Malone hadn't considered the drunks. He set a foot on the ground to steady himself. In the scant light from one flickering bulb, old Anghus's face shone as shiny and dark as a living bog body. Malone shook his head to rid himself of the illusion.

"Likely no one will venture close to the bog body," Anghus said, "but then you never know either."

"What's that you say?"

"It's *that*, up there asleep below the May tree. Themselves won't be liking visitors to the site, not tonight of all nights."

"Themselves," Malone scoffed. "May tree. That gnarly old hawthorn hasn't seen flowers in years."

"True," Anghus said. "Close on a decade now, to be sure."

Malone clutched the counter as he stood. "You're talking in circles, you old git. First, I'm to guard the place against drunks, then I'm to steer clear because of the thin veil. So which is it?"

Anghus shrugged and nodded for Fergus to pour another whiskey. He drank it down. "Best be on about it then."

CHAPTER THREE

Malone stumbled out of the pub after Anghus. "Where are we going?"

"Did I misunderstand ye? I thought you decided to guard the site during Samhain. Lore may be lore, but the bonfire revelries are true enough."

Malone knew Anghus was goading him, but his tongue refused to form a quick response. Instead, he followed Anghus through the village. Candles and lanterns placed in front of houses and shops illuminated plates of food left out as offerings to the gods. Villagers lurched past with gaping smiles and loud laughter, their faces orange and flickering in the glow, while old Celtic jigs blew around on the breeze. To Malone's surprise, the locals greeted Anghus like a celebrity with the men patting him on the back and the women hugging him. They ignored Malone, the comeover.

Anghus guided him with a nudge now and then as they left the central square and started up a cart track into the hills. Around them, the bonfires grew and moonlight glistened off the Irish Sea beyond the silhouette of Peel

Castle's fortifications. Malone swallowed against the smell of smoke. He hadn't been this drunk since one leave or another during the war.

"Bloody hell, man," he said. "Why'd you souse me in drink if you wanted me to guard the site?"

"You'll be all right. It was your idea, not mine."

Was it? Malone couldn't remember. In any case, he'd see to it that no one desecrated the site in an alcohol-fueled act of idiocy or Manxian pride.

A furtive expression flitted across Anghus's face. He'd gotten Malone drunk on purpose, no doubt about it. Probably had a Samhain prank in store for him in an attempt to scare him off the island. Let him try.

Malone grinned. "You're right, laddy. My idea. I'll guard the bog body with my fecking life."

Anghus raised his eyebrows. "Will you, then? I don't mind hearing that. Come along."

The dog howled again.

"There's old Moddey Dhoo with his invitation," Anghus said.

"Invitation to what?"

"To guard the bog body—did you not just say that?"

Malone opened his mouth and closed it again. The muddy cart path up the hill slipped and slid below his feet, but he kept on because the excavation must remain pristine. No drunks pissing into the trench and no one stealing his tools, that was for bloody sure.

They arrived at the site. Anghus peered at the sickly hawthorn rather than into the splayed bowels of the earth where the bog body had started to reveal itself.

"I suppose you'll be figuring it out sooner or later," Anghus said, "but take care with Caorthannach." His voice hitched. "My son—God rest his soul—must have mentioned the local tales." His arm shot out with crooked index finger aimed at the bog body that would make Malone's name. "The other world, where the likes of *that* should remain."

"Not likely," Malone snapped. "If you're so concerned about the other crowd, why help me with the excavation?"

"Keeping an eye, is all. Themselves have ways of protecting themselves."

Anghus vanished into the night, leaving Malone to a fire-tinted murkiness with just enough illumination for the hawthorn branches to cast spiky shadows on the ground. Malone plunked himself down next to the tree and, aided by his drunkenness, sank into a relaxed state of vigilance. He'd experienced his share of inebriated watch duties. Even a few times with Private Lonan Ward, Anghus's son.

The wind died back to reveal the tidal shush of the Irish Sea. The so-called phantom dog added its lament along with the dry rub and creak of old wood. Spring would arrive soon enough, and hopefully by then Malone would have settled how to transport the bog body to a lab back in Ireland for proper study and preservation.

After an hour, edginess beat out relaxed. The hawthorn's naked, twisting branches stuck out in all directions above him, grasping the darkness. A gust of wind bowed the branches toward him. They scraped against his jacket and their shadows jumped up at him from the ground. He jerked to his feet and lost his balance. A sulfurous scent disoriented him as he stumbled backwards into the trench. Howling and music and far-off human merriment faded into a flashback of artillery fire and screams.

"No!"

He scrambled to the edge of the trench and glared up at the hawthorn. Of all the plants on the planet, there was none he hated more than these raggedy old things. A weed, the common ingredient in every hedgerow on the island. He'd see about this being a wasted evening and tomorrow a wasted day. He picked up his trowel and a pick to start digging away the roots that hampered their progress.

A snakelike movement, black against more black, startled him. He clicked on his torch and swung it toward the bog body's feet. In the beam of light, they shone smooth as oil slicks. The big toes now touched each other as if the bog body had relaxed in sleep. Holding his breath, Malone leaned closer. A black bubble oozed out from under the nail bed, and with a pop that made Malone jump, dribbled down the toe.

He froze. "Jesus wept," he said, "this is—"

Impossible? Mindboggling? Both? His heart raced with excitement. This had to be a new development in the annals of bog body research. Condensation of some sort. The body settling now that it was exposed to air.

He pulled a notepad out of his inner jacket pocket along with a short pencil. He licked the pencil tip and jotted a few notes that he hoped he'd be able to read the next day. Too bad he'd forgotten his camera. As he wrote his observations, another slithering movement caught his attention. Malone angled the torch toward the feet again. To his dismay, the toes pointed toward the sky as before, with no sign of condensation.

He'd swear on his wise old aunties that the feet had shifted. He bent closer. Nothing. He was more drunk than he'd thought. Disappointment further fueled his desire for progress on the dig, especially because he suspected that Anghus and his men worked slow as a winter thaw on purpose. They should have uncovered the body up to the knees by now.

Well then, he'd just have to help them along, wouldn't he?

Malone climbed out of the ditch and returned to his pile of tools. He picked up a handsaw. The fact that lone hawthorns like this one were said to be faery trees—and beware to the person who harmed one—didn't phase

Malone. He had the excavation to think about. Never mind clearing away the roots, the whole bloody tree must go.

Four more bonfires had popped up around him, but this particular hillside remained dark. The ashy scent of smoke thickened, and figures silhouetted by bonfire glow writhed and entwined like the hawthorn branches. Malone shrugged off the tension that had gathered in his shoulders and strode up to the ailing tree. It was dying anyhow. He pressed the serrated blade edge against one of the main thrusting branches. The dog's howls rose into barking and laughter rose into cackles. Hawthorn branches clacked against each other like chimes made of bones. He tightened his grip on the handsaw. He'd seen too many bones in the war, heard too many body parts blown to gooey bits.

"Would you fecking stop," he ordered himself.

Malone pressed the saw blade against the hawthorn trunk and cut the first groove with a grind of metal teeth against wood. As he pulled back for the next stroke, clamminess wrapped itself around his ankle.

Chapter Four

Malone had predicted a prank, and here it was. He jerked his foot. "I'll brain you myself if you don't leave off," he called back. "Bloody bastards."

He continued sawing. A yank toppled him, causing him to hit his head against a branch. Dazed, he started to rise, but a jerk sent him sprawling forward onto his elbows. Malone grabbed for the hawthorn trunk, but another yank pulled him backwards toward the trench. The pressure encircling his ankle increased and moved up his leg. Closing his eyes against wooziness, he dug his fingers into the boggy ground. Clammy cold seeped through his jeans as he jerked his leg. The pranksters jerked back.

"You'd better watch yourselves," he said. "You don't want me for an enemy."

Another heave dragged him backwards. He gritted his teeth against a nightmare image that often infested his dreams. Disembodied limbs mounded in a squirming, worm-like mass that reconstituted themselves into a deformed version of a man. The dead did not rise, he reminded himself. This was his imagination plus the fecking whiskey and the leftover effects of battle fatigue that cursed his existence. This was the smell of bonfire smoke in the air—not enemy fire—and prankster locals—not enemy combatants come back to life.

"Stop!" he yelled.

His voice rang out louder than expected. The barking dog went silent, and voices and music faded into a tidal force from within the earth itself. A moist roiling and churning rumbled loud in his ears. The pressure around his leg intensified. Malone kicked out against the sucking, glutinous force that gathered behind him, but he remained powerless against the pull. His fingers etched drag marks into the ground.

He twisted around to grab for the binds that held his leg and felt tensile smoothness. Fibrous. Not fingers or cords, but roots.

He yanked at the roots' pallid mass that curled up his leg. The pressure increased, and the trench deepened and widened into a cavernous maw. His pulse beat loud enough to drown out the rumble of moving earth. With one mighty jerk from the roots, Malone rose weightless into the air; with the next jerk, the hole sucked him down. Roots soft and clingy as a woman's arms wound around him so he couldn't move. Struggling only caused the roots to tighten their grip. They contracted and relaxed, pushing him deeper and deeper into the earth's bowels. He expanded his lungs with air in the pauses between contractions and exhaled when the roots bore down on him again.

After what felt like an hour, the roots retreated. A queer glow surrounded him as he floated in a weightless place. Around him a cloud of spectral lights flickered. He felt his head in search of a lump resulting from his collision with the hawthorn. He had to be concussed.

He shifted around to see a man hanging upside down in front of him. The man's dark red lips stretched into a grin, and intelligence shone out of near-black eyes. Thin and pale, he wore black tie under a cape that defied gravity.

"Welcome," he said and flung out a hand like a magician performing a card trick. Dozens of images fluttered toward Malone. They resembled pictures that might appear on a deck of cards except that they hung in the air like three-dimensional hanging ornaments. The images scattered before Malone could interpret them.

"Better luck next time," the man said. "And may luck be with you, Malone Wolfe. This world does odd things to a man."

The man snapped his fingers and disappeared. Wind ripped past Malone as he fell. Moments later he landed with a swoosh on a jellied surface. His stomach arrived in close second along with a wave of nausea and a bout of retching.

Rather than a concussion—or maybe in addition to a concussion—perhaps Malone was riding the waves of one of his bloody waking dreams, in which he knew he dreamt but couldn't wake himself up.

"Had to be the bonfires," he told himself. And the smoke, and the scent of smoke. "I'm dreaming. I'll wake up."

Or perhaps he'd lost his mind at long last. He'd been warned. Hadn't he been warned? Nine months of recuperation in the hospital, prey to every trick of his mind. His mind, the ultimate prankster.

The jelly-like substance that had buffered his fall melted away. Malone raised himself to his knees, then to his feet. A stagnant orange glow with no source that he could pinpoint saturated the space around him. In the oddly useless and flat light, Malone sensed walls enclosing the space but not how far away they were. He stood in the center of a mosaic circle of multi-colored stones. Twenty feet in diameter, the swirling mandala-like design pulsed and shifted into new and elaborate geometries that curled in on themselves, an excitement of stonework.

Malone reached out and a stone spiral reconfigured itself into a serrated edge much like his handsaw. He jerked his hand back against his chest and then stretched his other arm out in the opposite direction. Another stony appendage whipped toward him and dropped back into the writhing design when Malone recoiled.

He craned his neck to squint into the oblivion above his head. No sign of the root system or hole through which he'd fallen. He closed his eyes. In the void where sound should exist, he caught the echo of air in his ears, the whisper of breath through his nose, and even, he thought, the crackle of his lungs as they expanded.

"This isn't real," he told himself. "This is a waking dream."

On a deep exhalation, he stepped forward. Stony tentacles struck out at him like cobras. He ducked and rolled to avoid the first one, only to have the second one latch onto his calf. He yowled but held his ground.

"This isn't real," he said.

He kicked out as he had when the roots dragged him into this place. The rock appendage broke apart and reformed again. Malone army-crawled through the colorful outgrowths that pummeled him from all sides. He lashed out with his arms and legs to no avail. Finally, he pulled off his jacket, stood, swung it around him, scattering rocks in all directions, and leapt the rest of the way out of the circle.

Malone rolled up his pant leg to display a circlet of puncture wounds around his calf. The pummeling had left him bruised and scraped, but, once again, this wasn't real. This was his imagination recreating the war in a most surreal fashion.

Or. A thought occurred to him as he pulled his jacket back on: Anghus drugged him. Malone had left his drinks a few times to hit the loo. He'd heard that a species of hallucinogenic mushroom grew on the island.

The thought had no sooner entered his head than a funnel of dancing lights floated toward him from the murky depths above. They fluttered with the resonance of hundreds of butterfly wings as they settled on the ground. A pinkish vapor rose and divided itself into the outlines of people. Or, not people exactly, but entities who slid into each other and apart with the same flat quality as the surrounding depthless illumination.

Dog howls approached. Malone swiveled to follow the dog's path, but it darted out of vision's reach. The howls grew to a deafening roar and a dark form rose out of the spectral crowd. A massive black wolf with yellow eyes like the bonfires padded toward him. Shadows shifted within its eyes, reminding Malone of fallen platoon mates who'd burned to a crisp with agonized cries that still filled his dreams.

The wolf leapt. Malone fell back a step, and a stony tendril latched itself around his calf again. A moment later, a whistling note clear and pure as a dew drop rang out. In response, the wolf altered course in midair and landed next to Malone with a snarl. Rock tendrils patted it as it trotted across the mandala to the side opposite Malone. The crowd of pinkish beings parted and from nowhere yet approaching all the same, a woman appeared to stand next to the waiting wolf.

Malone tried not to stare because he suspected that her beauty could devastate as easily as it could entrance. She stood fierce yet alluring, with long, black hair, a penetrating gaze, and a lithe strength to her stance. A shield centered on the chest of her flowing tunic reminded Malone of the stone mandala on the ground between them. She carried a golden staff sharpened at both ends. At her side sat the wolf that was no longer a wolf but a cuddly spaniel.

"Welcome, Malone Wolfe. Please excuse Moddey Dhoo. He's protective and gets lonely for companionship."

The Black Dog ghost of Peel Castle? Whatever dark terrain Malone had entered, for whatever reason, he wanted out now. "This isn't real," he said.

He turned away and bumped into a wall. The matte orange glow distorted his vision. He held out his arms but felt nothing, after all, and stepped forward only to bump into the wall again.

From behind him, the woman said, "You can't escape that way. Or in any manner you can imagine."

Chapter Five

Malone's waking dreams often mutated into nightmares, and when they did, he forced himself to wake up by closing his eyes, pressing fingertips against his temples, and shaking his head back and forth. "You're not real. I'm waking up now."

When he opened his eyes, the same flat glow surrounded him and the pinkish beings still shifted and merged into each other. Most of all, the woman with flowing hair and a warrior's stance observed him as if he were the artifact.

"You don't understand where you are?" she said.

"I'm nowhere."

"Nowhere is still somewhere. In this case, the other world."

Malone laughed. "Oh, for feck's sake. Now I'm being ridiculous. Anghus and his patter about the other crowd and the thin veil obviously got under my skin." He smiled, relieved. "The other world, that's rich even for me."

The pinkish blur of entities crackled and their voices like butterfly wing beats rose in pitch. The woman raised her palm in a graceful movement, and they subsided.

"Be careful what you mock, Malone Wolfe," she said. "You're here under duress."

"Is that right?" Malone might as well enjoy himself since his current state—whether drugged, dreaming, concussed, or insane—held him tight for the moment. "I'm at a disadvantage. Who do I have the privilege of speaking to?"

"I'm the mother of the being who has been resting at peace since before humans sowed their first grains of wheat."

Malone recalled the word Anghus had used for the bog body. "Caorthannach?"

"Ah," she murmured, "so you've heard this name."

Malone stood transfixed, unable to fathom this figment. He stepped toward her. The moment his foot landed, her staff stretched the distance between her and Malone without leaving her hand. Its point penetrated his clothing and pricked his skin.

"Do not approach me unless I bid you to do so. There are rules, and you've already broken enough of them."

"If this is the other world as you say, I'll need proof."

"The stone beating wasn't enough?" she said.

"No. I suspect I'll wake up or gain consciousness before things get too rough."

To prove his point, he stepped toward her despite the sharpened staff. He winced as the point sank into his skin. The woman raised her eyebrows but held her stance. He'd suffered worse than this, so he stepped forward again and felt the tip bury itself between his ribs.

"You'd kill yourself to make a point," the woman said. "You are a singular human man. So be it. Here's your proof."

Lowering her chin, she tightened her grip on the staff and pushed the tip through Malone's body. The pain electrified him and his mind floated beyond it and into shock.

The woman's staff shortened as she walked toward him. Her voice never lost its purity. "Now you are dying. Satisfied?"

"No," he mumbled. "I always wake up."

Malone sank to his knees. Each breath tasted like blood, and his eyesight shrank to a pinpoint. A buoyancy enveloped him, a kind of hovering between life and death that he recognized from his final trek back to his platoon two weeks after he was assumed dead or captured.

"You're real?" he said.

In a smooth and strong move, the woman withdrew the staff. Reignited pain blacked Malone out and when he resurfaced, he found her stooped beside him with palms pressed against the wound. Warmth enveloped him and the pain faded. He wiped away drying blood to see—nothing. Not so much as a pinprick where the staff had entered him.

His scientific brain scrabbled to make sense of this miracle, and in trying to make sense of it, he understood that he was sane, despite it all. His blood coated the golden staff, yet he was no longer injured. The woman had also healed the bruises and wounds left by the rocks, and the sore spot where he'd hit his head on the hawthorn.

Being Irish-born, Celtic lore and legend had saturated Malone's childhood thanks to his mother, a storyteller of the first degree. The Children of Lir and the Salmon of Knowledge, as well as assorted faery people. Like Grimm's fairy tales, the stories weren't meant to be believed, and as his tendency toward analysis and exploration had grown, he'd left mythology behind altogether. Yet, the woman before him would have him believe that the bog body was a member of the other crowd.

No. The bog body was an ancient artifact. Its grotesque size had a name: gigantism.

Malone rose and stepped away from the woman to gather his thoughts. If he'd crossed the veil into the other world—he still harbored the "if"—then he must stay calm and note his observations. He pulled out his notebook and pencil. The pencil went limp in his hand. With a flick of her fingers, the woman flung the pencil and pad into the haze of orange that had no depth and reflected back no surface.

"You like to break the rules," she said, oblivious to the blood that dripped onto her hand from the upended staff.

Moddey Dhoo appeared at her side. His curly spaniel ears perked in Malone's direction, but he remained at a heel beside the woman.

"You'll have to enlighten me about the rules," Malone said.

Her smile was a miracle, and her laughter a crystalline melody. "Indeed. One rule should be obvious enough by now. The *huath* shall not be harmed."

Huath. The old word for hawthorn that also represented the sixth letter of the Ogham alphabet used by the ancient Celts.

"Surely Anghus gave you fair warning about the *huath*," she said.

"You know Anghus?"

The woman walked around the edge of the mandala, away from him and then toward him again. Her hair floated around her in soft waves, and when she moved, an after-shimmer followed her. Her skin glowed as if she were the source for the odd luminescence that surrounded them.

"Bad tidings come to those who harm a *huath*," she said, "especially the one that protects my child. Unfortunately for you, you disturbed its sleep. Hopefully you will escape before it catches up with you, but the way is treacherous. Remember the mighty career waiting for you in the top world. Let that motivate you to complete your journey. Your ambition will serve you well here." Her smile lay sweet upon her, her voice soothing as honey. "Or maybe not."

"You're talking in riddles—"

"Quiet." She faced him with black eyes boring holes into him. "Moddey Dhoo shall accompany you. He'll be your faithful companion as long as you obey the rules."

A spy, in other words. Malone had entered another battlefield. Moddey Dhoo blinked at him with the same fathomless black eyes as the woman, except that deep within them smoldered embers of malevolence ready to spring out like exploding mines. With a force of will, Malone quelled his fear.

"What are the rules?" he said.

"That's for you to discover."

"Who are you?"

"I go by many names, but the common will suffice for now. The Tuatha addressed me as Danu, their mother, but they also referred to me as their Queen of Wands. You must find the Four Wands and pass their tests to free yourself of this place. Finding them may lead to your salvation."

Like Odysseus, Malone thought, who survived great trials in hopes of arriving home again. All this for harming a bloody hawthorn and disturbing the bog body.

"I suppose you and the rest of the other crowd will play the parts of the capricious gods and place obstacles in my way?" he said.

She jabbed him with her staff hard enough to draw blood again. "You owe us, and you shall pay one way or another. But, finding the Four Wands at least grants you the chance to live out the rest of your pitiful life on the top world again. You must find them before my son finds you." Her voice turned serene and sent chills up Malone's back. "I sent him to a safe sleep millennia ago for a reason."

"And what reason was that?"

"He was born out of my primal fires with a fierce hatred of your kind." She poked him with the staff again. "When awake, he threatens the balance between your kind and mine."

"So you're saying the lore of the Caorthannach is real," he said.

She tilted her head, considering him as if he were a bug that required flattening. "You have much to learn."

Around Malone, the pinkish beings lost what little form they had as they shrank back into flickers of light. One moment Danu stood before him, the next not. Her voice surrounded him, everywhere and nowhere. "In legend, the Caorthannach was also known as the fire-spitter."

Her voice grew faint within the flutter of lights. "Listen, my son awakens."

And fainter still. "Can you hear him?"

Soft as an echo of an echo within a seashell, Malone heard a rhythmic rubbing that was both dry and moist, like a snake coiling in on itself.

Chapter Six

The ambient glow surrounding the beings and Danu faded, returning Malone to a twilight murk. A part of him still rejected the reality of this place. The other world and the other crowd within the other world weren't real. Legend. Lore. Myth.

On the other hand, death had almost claimed him until Danu healed him.

The spaniel approached and sat at his side. He licked Malone's hand as if to say, *Come on.* Malone stooped and cradled Moddey's head. With a *yip*, the dog licked Malone's nose, keen intellect apparent in his gaze.

"That mistress of yours, she's a right fine ball buster, ay?"

The dog whined and his long, silken ears perked. Deep inside his eyes, tiny pinpricks of yellow reminded Malone of the dog's true purpose as his minder in this world.

"How about leading me to the first wand?"

Moddey's stumpy tale wagged. Malone stood with a sigh. Once again, the air in his ears was the loudest and only sound. Except for the dry rubbing sound. The bog man. Danu's son. Caorthannach. Fire-spitter. Most of all: artifact.

Time to move. He held out his hands and walked away from the stone mandala. The space had the feeling of a bunker, of entrapment. His breath caught in his throat, a spasm of nerves, before expelling itself. This was not a bunker, and the haze was not smoke.

His hands bumped up against a wall. Close up, the slick surface shone as mummified and smooth as the bog body. So smooth the material felt like nothing, if nothingness could be sensed by touch. Malone stored away the information in hopes of labeling this substance later. He let his hand lead the way along the wall. Moddey remained at his side.

"You're no help," Malone said.

His thoughts churned over Danu's enigmatic pronouncements. According to his storytelling mother, the "Tuatha" Danu had mentioned referred to the Tuatha Dé Danaan, ancient gods, that loosely translated meant "Children of Danu."

Right. That made a wee bit of sense, but proclaiming herself the Queen of Wands was a new one. Wands were implements for magic, and Danu had mentioned that four existed. Presumably, these magical implements would help him escape this place. More than that, though, magical implements would be priceless in what Danu had called "the top world."

A rush of anticipation coursed through him as he imagined his triumphant return to the top world with proof that the other world existed, only to be quashed by another thought. Danu had also accused him of owing them.

Malone swatted the back of his arm. "Ouch, what the—?"

He jerked around with fists raised in a pugilist's stance. A twinkling light hovered in front of him. One of the other crowd. Malone reached out to capture it. Instead, the faery zipped toward him, stung his neck and retreated.

"Hey!"

Another faery appeared, and then the two lights shot toward him. The number of twinkling beings doubled again to four, with four more stings. Then eight, then sixteen, each darting in to sting him. 32, 64 … Malone batted at them, knocking the stinging little faery bastards backward, which only made them multiply faster.

Moddey's ears flattened against the sides of his head. His fur bristled, and his hackles rose.

"Moddey, sic 'em," Malone said.

Instead, the dog locked eyes on him. The long silken ears grew tattered and the molten specks within his eyes brightened. He growled.

With outstretched arms, Malone ran headlong into emptiness in an attempt to escape the stinging. His feet made no noise as they pushed off the ground. The pricks like miniature pincers continued unabated. They doubled again and again, stinging his back and legs through his clothes. His feet cycled, and it took a moment for him to realize that they were no longer touching ground. Like a plane gathering momentum for takeoff, the wee bastards had stung him into running fast enough for lift off.

"Real cute," he said.

Wind batted his face, but otherwise, he had no sense of movement while he floated within their lights. After several minutes, the faeries flickered away and with a lurch, gravity reclaimed him. He fell through darkness. A blue shimmer kept pace next to him. Out of it the hanging man swayed toward him. Blood dripped off his chin in gooey rivulets.

He fanned delicate fingers in front of his face. "Pick an image, any image."

With each finger flick, an image in three dimensions flashed past Malone. He managed to snag one in midair, but it fluttered out of his grasp. A king or an emperor, gone before he could absorb the details.

The man opened his mouth in a meaty smile to reveal a couple of incisors that would do Moddey proud and disappeared. Insight flashed—Abhartach!—just before Malone landed with a thump that knocked the breath out of him.

Abhartach, the legendary tyrant who had been buried upside-down to prevent him from rising up to drink the blood of innocents. Scholars said he was the true inspiration for Bram Stoker's Dracula. Malone wasn't keen to gather evidence about him, to be sure. In fact, Abhartach made him more uneasy than Danu, or Moddey, or the bog man.

Groaning, Malone stood. Hundreds of tiny welts covered his skin, and each one felt home to a pricker that burrowed into his muscles. He hobbled a few steps and stopped. A vast plain carpeted with grass the color and size of fingers surrounded him. In the reddish haze, distances spread vast and illusory at the same time, as if he could pass a hand through a projected image of the plain. The space above his head couldn't be called a sky either; it was a dome of nonexistence to Malone's way of thinking. An empty space between dimensions.

A breeze bent the grass and whipped back Malone's hair. He sniffed but caught no scent; he listened but heard no rustling from the grass. Wincing against the welts, he stooped to collect a specimen that withered as soon as he plucked it.

A low growl startled Malone, and he whirled around to see Moddey. The movement sent hundreds of tiny torments ricocheting through his body. He froze at the sight of Moddey's curled upper lip. Malone was beginning to recognize the behavior. He'd broken a rule, as he had when he'd swatted at the faery bastards. If he wasn't supposed to harm a May tree, the same must hold true for the denizens of the May tree.

"What now?" he said to Moddey. "Is this sacred grass? Not supposed to collect proof of this place either?"

He dusted the remnants of grass from his hands and held them out to Moddey. Holding his breath, he placed a hand on the dog's head and felt him relaxing his vigilance.

"Well," he said, "where to now?"

The first wand must be hidden within this wretched terrain. It would help if he knew what he was searching for. Danu's magical implements could exist as anything from golden rings to more hawthorns to staffs similar to Danu's.

From beyond the low white noise in his ears, the snake-like slither of the bog man grew louder. "Where's the first wand? We need to get cracking."

The dog's ears perked and Malone searched the plain in the direction the dog's nose pointed. A structure stood a few miles away, and, clenching his jaw, Malone set off toward it. During the war, he'd marched with feet about to fall off from infected blisters, trench foot, you name it. He could do this.

Moddey fell in beside him. Each step ignited a thousand mini-agonies, so it took him a few minutes to notice the ground rolling faster under his feet than logic allowed, and within twenty minutes he stood before a structure that he understood. At long last, something tangible he could wrap his head around.

CHAPTER SEVEN

The portal tomb, or dolmen, that stood in front of Malone consisted of three limestone slabs—two verticals and a third capstone balanced over them to form a roof. Malone had studied plenty of them, but what struck him with an archaeologist's wonder was the immense size of this structure. Towering twenty feet above him and ten feet wide, a tomb worthy of a king. Or an emperor.

"Aah," he said to the dog. "Abhartach might have a purpose, after all. Hints."

Moddey sniffed within the structure and, finding it satisfactory, collapsed with a grunt and fell asleep. Malone wasn't fooled; any false move and the dog would be up and snarling. He followed Moddey into the dolmen and pressed his hands against one of the slab walls. The dog opened one eye and twitched his nose, but otherwise ignored Malone, which meant that touching this structure was allowed.

If this was a royal tomb, then the wand he sought might exist in the form of a bone relic or bejeweled treasure. His heart beat harder as he imagined securing proof of this place, of reading his name in all the journals. He'd find a way to smuggle evidence out of here without Moddey catching on.

Tensing against pinprick jabs from the welts, Malone knelt on the ground and pressed his hands into the fleshy grass. The blades withered beneath his fingers and palms, leaving hand prints in the dirt below. Once again, Moddey peeked and closed his eyes again. So, as long as Malone didn't collect specimens, he was safe. Maybe.

The fine, moist dirt crumbled out from between his fingers. He started digging while the scentless wind blew through the dolmen neither colder nor hotter than his body. The tiny faery welts continued to ache and soon his fingers chafed as well.

Malone dug until he'd widened a hole two feet square and a foot deep. He rested and raised his face to the wind that failed to cool him. He wiped the dirt off on his jeans but a crusty layer remained. He scraped at the residue, but it hardened like a plaster mold an artist might create. Or, like peat mummifying a body.

He rubbed his hands against the pallid grass, leaving streaks of dead blades. The dirt crust encasing his hands sent filaments twining up to his wrists and arms. He quelled anxiety with deep breaths and glanced around for a tool that he could use to crack off the shell. Nothing, not even a rock. He approached one of the slab walls and swung his arm like a bat. The bone-rattling impact made his head buzz, but the dirt shell remained intact.

Moddey rose to pace back and forth beside him. His head hung lower and his spaniel's tail stub had lengthened.

Malone held out one of his arms. "Bite it off. Come on, boy."

The dog continued pacing while the dirt seeped and hardened up Malone's arms. From far off, Malone sensed the bog man's struggle to free itself. Danu must have granted him the power of sight into her son's movements: the dry sift of the bog man's limbs gaining traction against the earth, muscles warming up, the pop of a stiffened knee joint flexing for the first time in millennia. A most diabolical way to remind Malone that death loomed.

"Holy hell, Moddey, help me out here."

The crust crawled into Malone's armpits and molded his arms in place. He willed himself to remain calm even as his breathing grew shallow.

"Danu?" he called. "Hello?"

A jumpy pulse in his neck throbbed. Dirt encased his shoulders now. The crust constricted his lungs as it seeped its way around his torso. He ticked off various symptoms of suffocation—dizziness, hyperventilation, confusion, increased heart rate, unconsciousness, cardiac arrest, brain death.

Black dots in Malone's vision swam and merged. His aching lungs spasmed as the dots merged into a vague outline. A woman. Danu again.

Her pure voice wafted through the dolmen. "You underestimate the gravity of your situation here in the other world. You must redeem yourself or die."

"Redemption for what?" he gasped.

In a far-off corner of his mind, a voice whispered, *You know already.*

Malone no longer felt the wind or his limbs. He swallowed a spasm of fear. Once again, entering battle, once again to face death and his weaknesses.

"You aren't here to collect specimens or smuggle treasures to the top world," Danu said. "Do you understand?"

He nodded. He hadn't survived the war just to die this way. Those last weeks, the four of them a forgotten watch detail on the front lines whose relief never arrived. Trapped in their dugout and undone by days of artillery shells shrieking overhead, the ground-shaking barrage setting them on edge. Lonan Ward the most barmy of them all with his tales of home.

"Remember then, fail the wands' tests, you die. Pass the tests before my son catches you, and you *may* survive to discover what fate has in store for you, if you're found worthy."

The wind sighed and Danu wavered in the red-tinged haze. She and the world shrunk into a pinprick that disappeared when Malone's oxygen-starved brain gave out on him.

CHAPTER EIGHT

A rosy glow against Malone's eyelids arrived first, then the sensation of a breeze across his skin. He floated in this state for a time before his lungs heaved and he jerked awake to find Moddey with front paws on his chest and ears perked in friendly fashion.

"You don't fool me, little spy."

Malone rolled out from under the dog. The dirt that encased his body had vanished, and the welts on his skin had faded. The sky told the same nothing story, with no light source, no shadow, and no depth. He couldn't tell how much time had passed. He lifted himself onto all fours and staggered to his feet. Moddey waited with his usual watchful air in place. His ears flopped over without the silky spaniel fur anymore, and his curly coat had grown coarse.

No more "ifs" about it; this was the other world with the old-style gods at work. Arbitrary, fickle, vengeful, brutish—even sadistic. Find the Four Wands. OK. Survive their tests. OK. Then as his reward *maybe* survive *if* he was found worthy.

"What the bloody hell is that supposed to mean?" he ranted at Moddey. "Passing the tests should prove me worthy of survival. Isn't that how these things work, for Christ's sake? This is for shite. I could still refuse to play her game."

Moddey's ears flattened against his skull.

"Sod off, you."

There had to be a hidden agenda at play, but he refused to consider Danu's game in terms of his own fate. He didn't believe in fate, therefore had zero to prove about his worthiness in that regard. Instead, he would focus on the four priceless wands and figure out his own game plan from there.

Malone swiveled away from the dog toward the hole he'd dug and fell back a step in surprise. In the center of the dolmen stood a five-foot high standing stone. He ran his hands up and down the carved grooves that decorated the surface. He recognized the series of tree-like symbols as the Ogham writing system of the Celts. The primitive letters climbed the stone with each letter represented by a vertical line with horizontal lines branching off it. The letters differentiated themselves by the number of horizontal lines that touched each vertical line and whether they pointed left or right, or intersected the vertical line.

It had been a few years since Malone had studied the Ogham system. He ran a finger over the grooves of the bottom-most letter on the stone, which would be the first letter in the message. Four lines pointed right off the vertical line. He closed his eyes and leaned his head against the stone. In this temperature-less place, the stone's cool smoothness helped him think.

Four lines pointing right. The letter "N." With his finger, he wrote "N" in the dirt. He continued this way, until he'd written two words that made no sense. Not in English. Not in Old Irish.

NKOXY JKGZN

"This is the utter bollocks," he muttered.

Next to him, Moddey sniffed the breeze with nose lifted and ears perked. He woofed, and a second later a thump shook the dolmen. The rock slab above Malone's head ground against the support stones. A sharp clatter rained down on the roof reminiscent of horse hooves prancing from side to side. The dolmen amplified the hoof beats into blasts of enemy artillery.

Malone gritted his teeth and hunched over with fingers digging into the dirt. Deep in his chest, panic trembled to life. Not artillery. Hooves. He racked his brain for a hoofed creature of Irish myth, but Moddey's woofs ricocheted off the walls, fracturing his thoughts. The echo chamber effect transformed his woofs into a medley of fifty hounds baying at once.

"Moddey, stop!" he yelled.

Moddey snapped his mouth closed and stared Malone down. The baying racket continued.

Malone scooted backwards so that his back pressed against one of the slab walls. The source of the baying racket came from the top of the dolmen. Dogs and a hoofed animal. An impossible notion entered his head. Another Irish mythology lesson from his mother.

The clamor of stamping hooves and dog cries increased. The yips, barks, and howls melded into a symphony, rising and falling to form a haunting whole out of which words emerged.

"You pride yourself on your intellect, but you understand nothing."

A warm touch slid across the back of Malone's neck. He swiped at a sticky substance on his skin as he peered around. Nothing there. The creature's hooves scraped the capstone as it shifted position. A dry rasp that reminded Malone of the bog man working its way free of its peaty imprisonment caught his attention. A forked tongue darted toward him around the lip of the capstone and whipped away again. Malone stood and clutched the standing stone to steady himself as a giant head descended and curled toward him. For a moment, Malone's mind froze, and then it screamed—snake!

The creature spoke through its baying voice. "You are not in charge here. Submit and you might survive."

Malone's tongue lay leaden in his mouth with the shock of beholding the questing beast of lore. Transparent membranes slid sideways across its eyes in a slow, considering movement. Its forked tongue shivered in and out of its mouth. The beast's head weaved closer. Smooth scales slid against the side of Malone's face. Malone held his breath against the swamp-like reek of the creature. One glistening black eye bigger than Malone's head bulged right in front of his face.

"Remember your father's laughter that long ago day," it said. "A May Day of your youth. How did that day land you here?"

"That makes no sense," Malone whispered.

"Does it not? You sat beneath a May tree that day. Do you remember?"

With a scrape of hooves against stone, the rest of the questing beast's body appeared. It landed on the ground and the beast's head recoiled toward a spotted leopard's body with the haunches of a lion and the legs of a deer. Its tongue whipped out once again and slipped itself around Malone's neck. The slippery noose of it tickled and chafed at the same time. Wooziness enveloped Malone. He sagged as memories floated up to the surface from that long ago day.

Eight years old. Three boys in their tatty paperboy's caps. They'd just graduated to long pants like Malone. "Mal-baby playing in the dirt again," one of them said as he grabbed an old paint brush from Malone's hand.

Malone's insistence that he was about to find a treasure was enough to roil them up into a frenzy of kicks.

Even then, Malone had longed to be an archaeologist, much to the shame of his father who considered it a useless, Anglo career only fit for traitors of the Irish cause. His father had many names for the English, one of his favorites being "those bastard fog-breathing Protestant invaders."

That day, the boys cracked three of his ribs and broke his nose, but he cried over the loss of the tools he'd managed to cobble together out of old dowels and a child's paintbrush he'd stolen out of the big family's garbage. When his father found him, he yanked him up by the arm and slapped him across the face.

"Big, brave archaeologist blubbering like a baby in nappies," he said.

He'd been drinking, of course, it being the first of May with celebrations that began as soon as the sun rose. He dragged Malone out into the square and pushed him into the ring of girls who danced around the maypole. "There's my wee girl," he yelled. "Get dancing, you, along with the rest of them."

Malone didn't dare disobey. The girls averted their gazes as his father guffawed from the sidelines with a booming baritone that never failed to entice others to laugh along with him.

"Not quite ready for long trousers, are you then?" he called out.

Malone weaved in and out of the girls, fumbling the complicated pattern of their routine, stepping on toes, lurching because of the jolts of pain from his ribs. What seemed like a lifetime later, he fled to the lone May tree on the hillside nearby. Its frothy pink petals mocked him with their cheerful beauty. He leaned against the trunk of the hawthorn, imagining himself uncovering treasures that would astonish his father.

The pungent scent of those long ago hawthorn blooms faded as the questing beast's tongue unwrapped itself from Malone's neck and he fell limp against the standing stone. The beast leapt with effortless grace onto the top of the dolmen. "Remember the May tree as you search for the Four Wands."

With a last crack of hoof beats on rock, the sound of baying dogs faded. In the quiet void, the crackle of the bog man's awakening continued to grow.

CHAPTER NINE

Moddey was all canine amiability as he stepped along with Malone to check the roof of the dolmen. Empty. Thank Christ. Malone's next thought revolved around regret that he hadn't ripped off one of its scales as evidence of its existence. His third thought was, Remember the May tree, my sweet arse.

The last thing he wanted inside his head was his childhood, but now thanks to the beast, it roosted there along with his accursed insights into the bog man's progress. The creature had loosened the peat enough to move its legs, which provided leverage to shift its hips, back and forth, up and down, to loosen the ground further.

Malone knelt and cautiously slung his arm around Moddey's shoulders. Ear flaps with short, coarse hair had replaced silken spaniel ears, and his cropped tail had grown into a whip-like appendage. Malone rubbed his hand along the dog's back, noting the coarser fur there, too. The glow in his eyes had grown bigger, but he sat calmly enough with tail lifting now and then in a small wag.

Danu had mentioned that the dog was lonely. Malone knew that feeling well enough. Had known it, he realized, since that moment under the May tree when he was eight years old and watched the rest of the May Day festivities from afar. However, remembering loneliness wouldn't help him decipher the Ogham letters. He returned to the standing stone to stare it into revealing its secrets.

NKOXY JKGZN

Danu and the questing beast had mentioned the number four. Four wands, four treasures he must find. He transposed the letters forward by four letters in the alphabet.

ROSBC NOKDR

More nonsense. Then he tried backwards.

JGKTU FGCVJ

Again, nothing.

Moddey woofed and ran out of the dolmen. Not again. "Come back here!"

Malone scanned the vast plain under its flat, matte sky that wasn't a sky and listened for hoof beats and dog bays. All remained silent except for the breeze whooshing through the dolmen. He followed the sound of Moddey's excited yips, wary but also intrigued to witness the cause of Moddey's puppy-like reaction. He circled the dolmen to find the dog cavorting around a young woman with white skin that glittered like fish scales in sunlight. Silky hair with a greenish tint hung down her back. She appeared to be naked, but the harder Malone focused his gaze, the more her skin shied away from view. He discerned her whole form only by gazing at the aura around her, but even then she was a mirage.

"Hello," she said without looking at him. Her voice rang like the sweetest of chimes after that of the questing beast. She fondled Moddey's ears and cooed at him. The dog had returned into his sweet spaniel form. He flopped onto his back, and she stooped to scratch his belly.

Malone waited, suspecting a surprise he might not like.

A moment later, she fulfilled his expectation. "I'm the Morrigan."

Ah, Christ. The Morrigan. From one dangerous female to the next. Or rather, from one dangerous female to three. The Morrigan were a trifecta of goddesses, and when one arrived the other two were sure to follow at some point. This one's beauty made for a bloody good disguise. The Morrigan had a tendency to strike with the neutral violence of nature itself.

Weary, Malone scrubbed at his face and backed away. Danu had no doubt sent her to distract him from discovering the first wand. Each wasted minute brought the bog man closer to finding him.

In front of the standing stone again, he stooped over the letters he'd scratched in the dirt. On the other side of the rock wall, the Morrigan hummed tunelessly. Moddey's grunts of pleasure as she rubbed his belly irked Malone. Unfortunately, the distraction was working. This time she met his gaze when he approached. Her eyes shone with the same iridescence as her skin.

"Which one are you?" Malone said. "Of the Morrigan. You're the three goddess sisters of war, if I'm not mistaken."

She raised an eyebrow. "For a stupid man, you're quite smart. I'm Nemain."

"Are you here to follow-up on what the questing beast said? Not that it was helpful."

"Oh? That's a shame. Maybe you're not that smart, after all."

She stood and glided past him with Moddey frisking around her legs. Malone caught up with her in front of the standing stone. She ran a hand up the stone, leaving an iridescent sheen on the rock that slowly faded away again. "The questing beast was trying to say that our battlefields live within us."

"Quit with the enigmatic malarkey. How do I decode the stone?"

Moddey growled and snapped at him. Malone stepped backward. Respect. He mustn't forget to show the proper respect.

Nemain continued on, undisturbed. For a war goddess, she acted oddly placid and serene, but then war goddesses must need their R&R, too. She circled the standing stone with fingers leaving their iridescent trail. "All in all, you performed well with the questing beast. I was taken with your memory of the May tree when you were a boy. Some battle scars remain with us, and family battle scars are often the worst. You entered the war with your scars leading the way. Your battles started that day under the May tree."

"Is that right? I'm more interested in talking about this standing stone."

She smiled, and the air around her glowed. The full force of her almost blinded Malone. He shielded his eyes with his hands. The glow of her condensed and darkened. "The May tree," she said.

A blue shimmer gathered round Nemain as her form dissolved into a raven and flew around the dolmen. Her bloodcurdling caws filled Malone with the horrors of war—wiping decimated flesh and brain matter off his face, stumbling over a dismembered leg, crawling beneath the corpses of his dead comrades to hide from the enemy. Nemain's caws were an omen, a prophesy of death, a warning of more horrors to come.

"What of helping me?" he called.

Her voice called back through the caws. "You're allowed six attempts to find the first wand. You've used two of them."

She shrank to a speck on the nothingness of sky. Unable to contain his frustration, Malone grabbed the standing stone. His bones rattled with the effort to throttle it. Moddey's growls rose over the sound of his own. He'd returned to his increasingly wolf-like form with a head that now reached Malone's thigh.

Panting, Malone backed away from the stone and sat in front of the letters he'd written in the dirt. He tried to ignore the stealthy noise of the bog man—the catch and release of its fingers scratching at peat, their slow but steady tunneling toward the surface—and failed.

"Moddey, come." The dog wasn't much of a comfort, but better than nothing as he sat next to Malone and let Malone stretch his arm around his neck.

Four more chances to decipher the code.

"Nice of her to warn me after the fact," he said.

Dried blood itchy on his skin reminded Malone that he could die right here, right now. He let his hands tremble, let the sweat drip down the sides of his face, let his body react to the danger while he considered the next number to use to transpose the letters. He could test all the possible permutations in his head, and how would the other crowd know?

Moddey's upper lip started to curl. Who was Malone kidding; they'd know.

His thoughts veered back to that day he was eight. Both the questing beast and Nemain had referred to this time in his life. "What about that day?"

Beltane, the spring festival on May first. Crouched under the blooming hawthorn while the villagers gathered in the field with their picnics and their music. Dancing caelis to welcome spring while pink petals like confetti flitted around him on the breeze.

May tree. Nemain had called the plant a May tree rather than a hawthorn. A crazy notion came to him, May being the fifth month of the year. He transposed the letters forward and then backwards by five letters, but the encoded message on the standing stone remained gibberish.

"What next?" he said.

Huath. Danu's word for the hawthorn, which also happened to be the sixth letter of the Ogham alphabet.

Two chances left. He exhaled long and slow and transposed the letters forward by six letters.

QTUDE PQMFT

Gibberish. His fingers trembled. One more chance. Next, he transposed the letters backwards by six letters.

HEIRS DEATH

A crack as loud as a thousand questing beast hooves startled Malone. Moddey clamped his jaws around Malone's arm and pulled him toward the plain of fleshy grass as another crack shook the dolmen.

Chapter Ten

Malone braced himself against Moddey as the ground rolled beneath his feet and the dolmen slabs ground against each other with a deafening squeal. A crack zig-zagged up the length of the standing stone. A shaft of light fierce and bright as bomb fire streaked out from the center of the stone. A moment later the standing stone split in half and collapsed.

Moddey dropped Malone's arm as the aftershocks petered out and the standing stone melted away as if it had never existed. Malone watched in fascination as the shaft of light solidified into a sword as luminous as the Samhain bonfires. The sword hung in the air, an implement fit for an emperor. The thick blade tapered to a point meant for thrusting. Graceful yet sturdy, with an engraved hilt that was both practical and decorative. Now here was an artifact worthy of the most prestigious lecture circuits.

With each step toward the sword, Malone peeked at the dog. He'd rather not grow the demonic yellow in Moddey's eyes further, that was for bloody sure. Moddey's ears remained perky. A good sign.

Malone laid a hand on the sword. Warmth stole through him, infusing him with the restorative energy of a fine meal and the comfort of a woman's touch. The hilt melded to his grip as he swung the blade around in a slow circle. He walked out from under the dolmen. The red haze that saturated the air burnished the blade with a warm hue.

Malone set the sword on the ground and bent closer to study the markings on the hilt. More Ogham. The first letter consisted of a horizontal line with two verticals pointing right. The letter "L." The next letter "I." Then "G." Then "H." And last, "T."

His heart jumped. *Light.*

His mind raced with understanding. Danu's Four Wands existed in the form of the four mythical treasures of the Tuatha Dé Danaan. He remembered his mother's bedtime stories about these treasures, a rare happy memory from an otherwise bleak childhood. One of them being the Sword of Light, which he now held. The other three: the Spear of Lugh, the Stone of Destiny, and the Dagda's Cauldron.

"Holy shite on a stick," he breathed.

He stroked the length of the blade, enraptured. No man could lose if he held this sword. All had to submit to the sword. It made an emperor of all who wielded it. With this blade, he could lop the head off the questing beast if it dared to appear again. He could take on the bog man,

Danu's son. And perhaps Danu herself. He could leave this infernal other world.

Malone picked up the sword again and tucked it under his belt so that it hung down the side of his leg. Awkward, but manageable.

"Now for the second wand," he said to Moddey.

He surveyed the landscape in search of hiccups in the terrain—lumps, holes, cracks—that could point him in the right direction. Unfortunately, all directions appeared identical in the undifferentiated landscape. The great plain ended in fuzz with no horizon line, just a seamless continuum into a reddish sky that was not a sky.

He decided to leave in the same direction from which he'd arrived. He positioned the dolmen at the correct angle behind him and walked away. Twenty minutes later he stopped and turned around, expecting to view the dolmen as a far off reddish blob of stone.

Fifty yards away, the dolmen hunkered patiently, a tomb in waiting for an emperor. Perhaps for Malone himself. No. Not that, even if Abhartach had shown him a king or emperor, and he now carried a sword worthy of a king or emperor. Yet, the message *heirs death*—there must be a connection. Royalty, heirs ... Or more likely one heir with the "s" indicating the possessive. *Heir's death.*

He walked backwards. The dolmen shrank in size as logic dictated it should. He pivoted away and back. Once again, the dolmen sat but fifty yards off. Perplexed, he returned to the dolmen. Retrieving the Sword of Light had granted him nothing. No divine favors, no glimpses into his so-called fate, no hints about how to find the next wand.

"The other crowd is messing with my head," he said to Moddey.

The ever-present slither of the bog man grew louder, more certain, the more time he wasted walking and talking to himself at the dog. Perhaps he was supposed to know what *heir's death* meant. Perhaps he was an heir because he'd found the sword. If so, the heir to what was the question. People had called Britain's new, young queen the "heir to the throne" for years.

He shook his head. He couldn't be an heir. That would be absurd. Wouldn't it? Besides which, the full message spoke of the death of an heir, which begged the question of whether he was an heir who was doomed to die rather than inherit.

In the top world, he was his father's heir along with his younger sister Maggie. His father threatened to disinherit him every other week but had yet to follow through. In the end, Malone held status as the male child and a decorated war hero, which only meant that he'd survived his childhood and survived the war. He didn't understand how these facts could possibly relate to the Ogham message.

Moddey's whip-like tail thumped the ground, and his ears perked. He woofed a greeting.

"What now?"

Malone was almost afraid to look but checked behind him anyhow to see another one of the little faery bastards. He knew better than to swat at it. "Go away!"

A second member of the faery folk brigade popped into view, and then two more, and then four more. They hovered over Malone's head, and when he moved they whipped down as one unit and stung his scalp. Malone ducked, and staying low, attempted to army crawl out of the dolmen. Moddey's growl stopped him in his tracks.

By then, hundreds of them had gathered above his head. Their glow lit Moddey's black fur with purplish highlights. In waves, they darted toward Malone and stung him about the face and shoulders until he flattened himself on the ground with arms covering his head. "I'm as low as I can go," he called out.

In desperation, he flung dirt at the wee bastards, hoping the dirt wouldn't encase him again. The pricks slowed. His body tilted as the surface gave way. One second he was sliding into a sink hole, the next, he landed on hard-packed dirt with a bone-jarring thump against the back of his head. He moaned and waited with his eyes closed until the pounding in his skull receded to a dull throb. He was fine, but the landings were growing rougher with each ride.

He rolled onto his side and remained that way for longer than necessary, because he already knew who'd greet him when he opened his eyes: Abhartach. He felt for the sword hugging his leg and laid his arm over it. Its warmth soothed him. He opened his eyes onto what appeared to be a tunnel and Abhartach dangling above him. Blood dripped from his jaw onto Malone's arm.

Malone jerked away and drew the sword out of his belt as he sat up. "In the name of the Sword of Light, I command you to keep your distance."

Abhartach's smile never wavered. He unfolded his arms from around his chest. He had delicate, pale hands. He held one of them up, opened his mouth, and bit the meaty area at the base of his thumb. He moaned with pleasure and his eyes rolled shut in ecstasy. To Malone's disgust, Abhartach squirmed as he sucked on himself and shuddered to a stop a minute later.

"Aah," he sighed. His red-tinged gaze settled back on Malone.

Malone's stomach churned. He held the sword higher, willing himself not to retch.

Abhartach's smile turned gloating before he exhaled a fountain of blood that floated in droplets and merged into one another. Images broke free of the blood and flocked around Malone. He grabbed for the closest one—a windmill—but it disintegrated along with the rest of the images.

Abhartach fanned his fingers as if he'd completed a fancy card trick. "Wheel of fortune seals your fate."

"Off with you, you perversion of nature," Malone said. "I don't believe in fate."

"I suggest you start."

Abhartach shot up into the darkness. Malone sagged with sword still raised. The sword's glow reflected back millions of glints that upon closer inspection revealed themselves to be cut diamonds. The other world's version of a bank vault. Enough wealth to finance digs for the rest of Malone's career.

Glancing around, he dug a nail beneath one of the jewels and dislodged it with a satisfying *pop*. The tunnel glittered like a starry sky into infinity. He pried another diamond from the wall. He was so entranced by the riches filling his pockets that he missed the shush of padding paws until Moddey jumped up on his back and knocked him to his knees. He circled Malone to face him with teeth bared. The yellow glow illuminated half of Moddey's irises. His ears now stood erect rather than floppy, and the fur on his tail had thickened.

Malone swung the sword so that its tip rested within an inch of Moddey's nose. The dog butted the sword aside with his head. Malone raised the blade again, but this time the sword refused to obey him. Malone grunted as he pulled and pushed the sword to no avail. As soon as Malone gave up, the sword allowed him to swing it back toward himself.

"What use is a sword if I can't use it?" Malone emptied the pockets of his leather jacket. "Satisfied?"

Nothing for it but to pick a direction. He decided on right since Moddey had arrived from that direction. A moment later, he overrode himself. What was the point? He'd end up where the other crowd wanted him anyhow.

He slid down the wall and laid the Sword of Light across his lap. He might as well rest and conserve his energy. At the moment, he couldn't sense the bog man. Maybe it needed a rest, too. Besides which, walking led nowhere, days never ended, and time and space felt fluid.

Moddey settled in beside him. The fairy welts jabbed at him, and his head still throbbed. Nevertheless, Malone's eyelids drooped. Maybe this was what the questing beast had meant by submitting. Submit to his body's need for sleep despite the unknowns that plagued him. Submit to the fact that he wasn't in control of what the other crowd planned for him.

He hoped submission was that easy.

CHAPTER ELEVEN

Malone jerked awake with an adrenaline surge that made his fingertips tingle to find himself lying on a ledge about twenty feet above another plain. Rather than fleshy grass, a shimmering blanket of sparkles covered the ground and reflected up to a silvery sky that, once again, was not a sky. More like a vast dome.

Here and there, shining houses and barns sat on parcels of land crisscrossed with dry-rock walls. They were constructed from the same glittering material as the ground. The sheen of prosperity almost blinded Malone.

He patted the Sword of Light. "You're at home here."

Moddey leapt in a graceful arc off the ledge and landed with a tail wag at odds with his glowing eyes and predatory stature.

"You like this place too, eh?"

Malone secured the sword in his belt, and with a twist, lowered himself off the ledge so he hung by his fingertips. He dangled for a moment. Closing his eyes, he prayed for a soft landing and released his grip. He was in luck this time. The ground compressed beneath his weight with an odd buoyancy. The glittering material beneath his feet reminded him of tightly woven chain mail. Flexible but solid at the same time.

"Lead on, Moddey. We're on for the second wand." Moddey dropped his haunches to the ground. "Fine, be that way."

Malone headed toward the closest house. He inventoried his body as he went. The burning sensation from the welts had receded, and his head no longer ached. All told, better than expected. He walked, lost in thought, and when he glanced up again the house no longer stood in front of him, but to his left. He altered course toward the building, but the edifice kept slipping away from him.

He squinted against the kaleidoscopic effect of the shining surfaces bouncing light off each other. Malone continued on and pretty soon the house slid out of sight beyond his peripheral vision. When he swung toward the house again, it sat sideways and above him on the chain mail ground. The slope of the ground equaled the slope of the dome above his head, one sliding into the other, and he now stood on a silken surface that his senses told him was the sky.

This was no dome; he stood within a sphere with no ground and no sky except for what his mind understood to be ground and sky. And at this moment his mind insisted that he was standing upside-down. Gravity at work in all directions defied what logic and his senses dictated to be true. What he'd taken for a horizon line sloped away from him on a diagonal. At any moment, he could plummet head first onto the "ground" that was the new sky that wasn't a sky at all.

Malone tucked his head and closed his eyes, willing himself to feel right side up. My feet are on the ground, he told himself. I'm grounded.

A wave of nausea rolled through him. His mind quailed in desperation for a horizon line that remained horizontal, and for his body to be positioned upright in relation to it. With eyes clamped shut, he dropped to all fours and crawled toward the chain mail surface that at least bore a resemblance to ground.

Beneath his ragged breaths, Moddey's steps at his side, and the shush of his jeans against the silken silver sky, Malone caught the sound of distant pops. The pop of the bog man's ten monstrous fingers as they found air for the first time in millennia. Breaking the surface—*pop*—with mummified fingernails—*pop, pop*—that had continued to grow over time—*pop, pop, pop*—into hooked claws. *Pop, pop, pop, pop.*

He pressed the heels of his hands against his temples in an attempt to massage equilibrium back into his head and then continued crawling with eyes closed. The far-off popping continued unabated. He hummed a nonsensical tune as he stretched one hand forward against the sky that wasn't a sky, then the next, then each knee. The popping took on a rhythm beneath Malone's hums.

He paused. Not the bog man anymore. Galloping hooves struck the metallic surface.

"Jesus, no," he muttered, "not the questing beast again."

The beast had nothing good to say, and he'd already said enough anyhow. Malone continued crawling. If he was lucky the bloody beast would gallop past him.

His hands landed on the chain mail. He sighed with relief. He sensed Moddey beside him, felt the hoof beats reverberating through the metallic mesh. He peeked and closed his eyes again. The silk sky curved away from him in one direction and the silver ground in another. In the distance, a black speck moved toward him.

"Moddey, sic 'em," Malone said.

Moddey growled in response. Malone had attempted that command previously, but Moddey wasn't his minion. If nothing else, Malone understood this by now.

He continued forward until he was well within the mesh half of the sphere. When he judged himself to be steady enough, he rose to his feet and opened his eyes. He teetered with vertigo but forced himself to keep moving in the direction of the houses. One of them appeared within his peripheral vision, canted sideways up the curve of the non-horizon to his left. The house would provide a decent defense position against the galloping beast. Not the questing beast, he could tell now, but that didn't alleviate his alarm.

How to reach the house? The direct approach caused it to retreat. Malone stepped sideways one step to the left and walked forward a few steps. He kept the house on his left and took another sideways step in that direction. And another. And walked forward again.

The beast took on the form of a sleek black horse. It galloped at an angle to Malone's right, growing closer even as it seemed it would pass him by. Malone increased his pace to a sideways trot. To his relief the house grew closer on a curving path from the left. He weaved sideways and forward with his left side always angled toward the house. The magnificent steed with streaming mane and tail curved toward him, close enough that Malone caught sight of the sulfurous amber glow of its eyes and smoke coiling out of its nostrils.

Malone ran. The house stood almost in front of him now. A simple cottage with two windows on either side of the front door. The horse was almost upon him, a scant few degrees of curve away from trampling him. The threshold into the house stood twenty feet away. Malone ran forward a few steps, trying to judge the proper angle to reach the door. It took all the will he had not to charge toward the doorway directly. He knew the second he faced the house head-on it would veer away from him.

Forward two steps, then two more to the left. He was heading toward the corner of the house now. He stepped left, and left again, and forward toward the window to the right of the front door. The smoke from the horse singed his hair. He leapt forward once more until he was only a few feet from the window, and then leapt left three times and fell into the house.

The horse reared. Its hooves scraped a wall in a shower of sparks. The house swayed. Malone scrambled to right himself and face the doorway. He pulled the sword from his belt. Its light bounced off the metallic walls with dizzying effect. His eyes watered, but he raised the blade.

Moddey stood in the doorway with perked ears and fluffy tail curled over his back. The horse stood twenty hands high with rippling muscles and coat glossy as obsidian. Sparks flew in all directions as it pawed the ground with shiny black hooves.

"You walk a crooked path, *duine*."

Malone recoiled from the sound of the horse's deep and resonant voice. A talking black steed could only be a pooka. According to his mother's tales, pookas were dangerous when provoked, unpredictable, and prone to vindictiveness, trickery, and shape shifting. Hobgoblins by any other name.

"My kingdom for a questing beast," Malone muttered.

"I heard that," the voice boomed. More sparks rose as the pooka banged the wall with his hooves. "Come out, *duine*, before I drag you out by your fifth limb."

A shiny black hoof smashed through the window. A moment later two hooves bashed in the wall. Part of the roof crashed to the ground with a cymbal-like boom. The pooka's equine head poked through the hole with steam jetting out of his nostrils. His eyes glowed like suns viewed through firestorms.

Malone held up the Sword of Light. "Stand back. All submit to the sword."

"You think it's that easy?" The pooka snorted. "You're a most foolish *duine*."

Malone remembered the word *duine* now. Old Irish for "human." He was a no-name human now. He lowered the sword, wondering why he bothered with it other than to smuggle it to the top world.

Moddey ambled toward the pooka with wagging tail.

"Traitor," Malone said.

On the other hand, inciting a pooka wasn't in his best interests. He followed Moddey out of the ruined cottage. The pooka's tail flicked and sent a breeze toward Malone.

"Which wand do you represent?" Malone said. "Are you here to help me find the next treasure of the Tuatha Dé Danaan?"

"Questions, questions." The pooka tossed his head and sidled sideways. "Look at this place, the world you rendered. Wall-to-wall treasure to go with your avaricious mind."

"I didn't create this place."

"Oh, but you did. Behold the reflecting pasture, only yours isn't flat." The stallion gazed around. "Shining surfaces with no soul. Barren earthly delights. Crooked as you are."

For some reason, the pooka's amber eyes brought to mind the stench from the befouled dugout and the decaying body of one of his watchmates lying nearby with an unseeing gaze aimed in his direction. The sense of being watched by the dead had spooked Malone into darting out of the dugout to cover the face with a cloth.

Malone shook his head to rid himself of the memory. "I don't know what you want from me."

"You will soon enough."

Chapter Twelve

The stallion grabbed Malone's jacket with his teeth and swung Malone aboard his broad back. Malone's legs stuck out like a child's. Moddey jumped up to sit behind him. Malone grabbed the mane as the horse galloped toward the silken sky that was not a sky. Malone closed his eyes when the hoof beats softened against the silken surface. He pictured them sideways on the sphere, heading toward upside-down. He swallowed and exhaled on the count of ten to ease his heart rate.

Ten minutes later, the light filtering through his eyelids grew softer. The pooka's hoof beats slowed to a canter and then to a bouncing trot. He reared and Malone slid off his rump. Upon hitting the ground, he rolled over and retched up bile. His stomach felt like it had shrunk to the size of a coin. He placed his hand on the sword. Still there, but the feeling of wellbeing and satiation it had granted him was long gone.

They'd arrived in a glade protected by towering maples and oaks. For the first time since Malone's arrival, scents other than Moddey's dog breath or the questing beast's reek tickled his nose. He floated in them for a moment, delirious. Tree bark, dewy undersides, mushrooms, and the lush carpet of grass he lay on. He relished the sounds of flies and leaf whispers and chittering squirrels. The crisp, clean scent of water within the fecundity of grass and trees propelled him to his feet.

The pooka grazed with tail swishing back and forth. He raised his head. "Welcome to my reflection. Your pasture was an awful illusion. The worst I've encountered yet."

Malone's throat rubbed like sandpaper and his tongue stuck to the roof of his mouth when he spoke. "Other *duine* have visited the other world?"

The pooka tossed his head. "Of course we've hosted others of your kind. They're usually innocents here by mistake. The reflecting pasture lulls them into a sense of safety until we return them to the top world. Most of the time, they experience their homes or other places that comfort them. We have ways of dealing with corrupt reflections before sending those *duine* back. Depending on what they reflect, we teach them a few lessons and hope they heed them on the top world." The pooka's snort hinted at gleeful cruelty. "And you? You're beyond special. You're damned, but perhaps you'll survive."

Malone wasn't in the mood for more dire proclamations from the other crowd. He lurched away from the stallion and toward the sound of water within the trees.

Every cell in his body screamed for hydration. He felt like a sucked-out shell, robbed of his life force by the reflecting pasture.

A stream like an azure ribbon danced and trickled through the trees. Moddey was already there lapping up his fill. Malone dropped to his knees beside the dog. As soon as he dipped his hands into the perfection that was this water, Moddey growled. His ears flattened against his head, and his upper lip quivered. His fangs were now the size of daggers. Malone dipped his head to drink out of cupped hands. The growling increased. Moddey snapped at Malone's arm.

"Good dog, Moddey," said the pooka.

Instead of a stallion, a creature with greenish, lumpy skin and bulbous, bloodshot eyes the color of mud appeared. He stood about four feet high with thick limbs and a barrel chest. The only thing cute about him were his floppy rabbit ears. His gaze glinted with sly intelligence. With a smile, he sidled up to Malone, dipped one of his thick hands into the water and sipped. Moddey continued growling.

"What will you take in exchange for water?" Malone said.

"You're a fiend for commerce." The pooka licked his fingers. "You'd strike a deal for a drink of water. How about a little common courtesy instead? You're a visitor in my home, after all."

"Oh." Malone felt like a fool. "May I drink from your stream, pooka?"

The hobgoblin nodded his head in majestic fashion. "Of course. Thanks for asking. You may call me Ilios."

Malone's body surrendered to—something—when he dipped his head to drink again. A swoon of pleasure, perhaps, or more like perfect oblivion. His hands floated in water the temperature of the Mediterranean, buoyant and perfect. He longed to become one with the water itself. Life would be perfect in the sheltering stream. He'd sleep the sleep of children with no regrets.

Ilios's ears twitched toward him like miniature weather vanes. "What regrets?" he said.

Malone continued drinking. The water soaked into his parched cells, but that wasn't enough. He felt dirtier than his dirtiest days trapped in the dugout. He submerged his head in the water.

"Hey," Ilios said and tugged at his jacket. "You'll pollute the stream."

Malone shrugged him off and sank his shoulders into the water. He opened his eyes to pure blue comfort. "I need a bath." His words rose up within bubbles and popped on the surface.

"I forbid you," Ilios said. "Moddey, attack."

Malone pushed off the bank, rolled over, and floated below the surface blinking up into a perfect blur of trees through the surface ripples. Ilios's squeal of anger barely penetrated his contented state. He couldn't remember the last time he'd experienced happiness with the world as it was. Even the dig for the bog man—the thrill of uncovering the first sign, a large toe—didn't compare to this. His satisfaction a fleeting sensation too soon pushed aside by thoughts of the future and denial of the past.

He floated toward the center of the stream with eyes closed. When he opened them next the water had darkened. A cramp convulsed him. He coughed and ingested water. A slimy strand of algae caught his leg. The water darkened further. He kicked toward the bank where Moddey and Ilios—now back in his stallion form—stood. Moddey's eyes glowed and his hackles rose.

Sickly grey ribbons of muck filtered past Malone. He coughed again and sank below the surface. The sting of inhaled water startled him. He rose again, coughing harder. The algae gripped him and jerked him underwater. When his feet brushed the stream bed, he kicked off hard, breaking the algae in the process. He surfaced with a sputter and much flailing.

Ilios reared and lunged into the water to grab Malone with his teeth. With one flick of his great head, Malone launched into the air and landed on the loamy bank. The next second, Moddey chomped down on his shoulder. Agony ripped a hole through Malone's core. He screamed. Moddey shook Malone as if he were a rag doll. Muscles tore away from bone, and the bones within his shoulder cracked.

"Moddey, stop!" a new voice called.

Moddey's jaws unclamped and Malone's second scream echoed off a million leaves.

Ilios's voice rose. "There I was, being hospitable for a change, and he infested the stream with his *duine* nastiness. No one's ever done that, ever. Look at it!" He wailed in despair. "It's not my reflection anymore. It's his!"

Rather than the purest of Mediterranean blues, leaden gray ripples now washed onto the bank, leaving a sludgy residue. Bubbles puffed along the surface and burped open with a stench like betrayal.

"He's a pestilence," Ilios said. "Kill him!"

The woman's voice murmured. Through the pain, Malone could make her out—Nemain?—as she stroked Moddey's head. The glow in Moddey's eyes left nothing but black rims around his irises. Malone shuddered. Wolf, definitely more wolf than dog now.

"You should have ordered Moddey to rip him to shreds!" Ilios said.

The woman stooped in front of Malone. "I think not."

"Nemain of the Morrigan?" he said.

"I'm Macha, her sister."

Through a fog of pain, Malone caught her darker blue sheen that reminded him of the sparkle within sapphires. She was twilight to Nemain's dawn. He had a vague recollection of her tendency to rain down blood and fire on her enemies.

His teeth chattered. "Can you heal me?"

"*Duine*," Ilios hissed. He had morphed to his misshapen hobgoblin form again. He strode up to Malone and slapped him. The movement sent shockwaves through Malone's body.

"Listen to him," Ilios said. "All about himself. A selfish and uncaring creature."

Macha tore open Malone's clothing to reveal bone glistening stark white against mangled flesh. The sight reminded him of the second man from his dugout to die. Raving with trench fever, he'd snuck out in the middle of the night and shot himself, leaving Malone and Anghus's son Lonan to fend for themselves behind enemy lines.

Macha closed Malone's clothing over the wound. "You do this to yourself. You succumb to your warped reflection with the ease of a fish into water. But not to worry, if you survive, your reflection will surely change."

"That's all well and good, but right now it's a problem," Ilios said.

"True, but we can't interfere with the process."

Process? What process? Malone groaned as much from pain as from frustration. The other crowd spoke in riddles, and he was tired of it.

Beneath the stream's belches, Malone recognized a new sound—a glutinous sucking as the bog man raised itself to a sitting position with sunken eye sockets and perfectly preserved and twitching eyelids. Malone shook his head against the visuals that rose up in his mind, unbidden.

"He deserves death," Ilios said.

Macha stood. "Perhaps so, but it's not for us to help that along. You're free to take him now."

"What?" Malone said. "I don't think so."

Ilios's smile of glee showed off a mouthful of crooked teeth. "Oh, yes, and what fun we shall have. Stupid, *duine*, don't you know you shouldn't anger a pooka?"

Chapter Thirteen

A blue shimmer swirled around Ilios, and a moment later he stepped out of it in his equine form with sulfurous gaze intelligent and calculating. He nickered and once again flung Malone into the air. Malone landed on his back and started to slide toward the ground. His shoulder went molten with pain.

"Stay on," Ilios ordered.

Malone righted himself and grabbed Ilios's mane with his good arm. The pooka took off at a gallop. Each stride shot agonizing jolts through Malone's shoulder. Ilios's verdant home petered out into the fleshy grass plain. The terrain appeared to be the same plain at least, but Malone could be miles away from the dolmen. Ilios slowed to a walk. Malone sank into a stupor. Sometime later he roused himself to the same silty reddish glow and sky that was not a sky. The only difference was his elevated viewpoint. Rope encircled his body and bound him to a hard surface about thirty feet above the ground. He had no memory of arriving, much less being trussed up like a hog.

Careful not to jostle his shoulder, Malone craned his neck to see a rickety windmill blade, a rotor hub and above that another blade jutting into the air. More blades stuck out of the rotor hub at different angles, five in all, wood grey with age and mossy in places. Abhartach had called it the wheel of fortune.

Jaunty whistling drew Malone's attention back to the ground. In his hobgoblin form, Ilios strode out of the millhouse that housed the windmill machinery. Moddey followed him. The wolf stood the same height as the pooka with glowing eyes all too visible.

"Perfect," Ilios announced. "Fair warning. Don't struggle because the windmill is on the brink of falling apart. But then again, if you fall, then you fall. What do I care?" He bit on his thumb, thinking. "No, that would defeat the purpose. So I order you not to struggle."

Malone could barely follow what Ilios was saying through the torment pulsing out of his wound. "Where's the Sword of Light?"

"Speak up," Ilios called. "I can't hear you."

Malone cleared his throat and tried again. "Where's the sword?"

"It's safe, have no qualms about that."

"What do you want? I thought I was supposed to find the next wand."

Ilios gurgled and then roared with laughter. His maniacal mirth made Malone squirm against the chafing ropes. "That's why you're here. Nothing's changed except that I've decided to add a dose of torture to the mix. You polluted my stream. For that, I've injected extra fun into the game by tying you to the windmill."

Malone had forgotten why he'd thought slipping into the stream was a good idea, except for a sensation of freedom from himself for those few minutes. "I apologize," he said.

"Apologies won't bring my spring back. I spent years perfecting it. Now I have to start from scratch again."

"Tell me what I need to decipher," Malone said.

"Decipher?" Ilios waved his hand. "Oh, no. No, no, no. We're beyond that. You'll ask me three questions—"

"What, why?"

"Whoopsie, you've lost one of your questions, *duine*. Really that was two, but I'll count it as one. In exchange, I'll ask you questions back."

Again with the belated rules. First, Nemain. Now, Ilios. At least Nemain had wanted to help him. Ilios was another story altogether.

Malone phrased his next question as a statement. "You have to answer truthfully, too."

"I must answer," Ilios said. "Those are the rules."

"Pookas aren't known for following the rules. You play tricks."

Ilios cocked his head. "Weelll, true enough. I guess you'll have to find out either way."

"You haven't said what happens to the loser."

Ilios rocked back on his heels. His smile turned fulsome. "If I lose—which I won't—I must reveal the next wand to you. If you lose—which you will—I leave you here for the one who should remain asleep to find."

"By losing, you mean—"

The hobgoblin bared his overlapping teeth in a snarl that reminded Malone of the wolf. He stamped his foot. "Answer the bloody questions and be consistent about it!"

That seemed easy enough. Too easy. Malone opened his mouth and shut it quick before another question popped out. He squirmed within the ropes, but a warning creak froze him. Pain engulfed his shoulder and Malone clenched his jaw against crying out when the windmill shuddered and with a grind of gears began to move.

"You don't like rides?" Ilios said.

The pressure of the ropes bit into Malone's injury as he rose and then stopped with his head pointing toward the ground. His head started to throb. The ropes slipped and caught, and the movement sent hellish waves through Malone's body. He refused to give voice to them. He wouldn't give Ilios the satisfaction.

Ilios paced back and forth in front of Moddey, muttering to himself with ears twitching this way and that, and then with a satisfied grunt pivoted toward Malone with a raised finger. "Question number one! Is there anything in your pockets?"

The windmill started up again, easing the pressure on Malone's head but torturing his shoulder again. He swung through the bottom position and started up again. Once again, the windmill stopped him with his head aimed at the ground. Black dots danced in front of his eyes. He'd forgotten Ilios's question.

"I'm not giving you all day," Ilios said. "Should be easy enough answer. What's in your pockets?"

"Lint, I have lint in my pockets!"

Ilios pursed his lips and nodded with eyebrow raised. A dramatic pause, and then he shouted, "Wrong!"

The shimmering blue light swirled around Ilios. A moment later, he appeared as a black and white jackdaw. Cackling with mirth, he flew toward Malone and landed on his feet. A moment later, rodent claws scurried down his leg and burrowed between the ropes. The movements tickled as Ilios nosed his way into Malone's pockets.

"Found it," Ilios said, and a moment later talons pushed off Malone. As a jackdaw again, Ilios landed and within the blue cloud transformed back into his hobgoblin form. He held out his hand. A perfect diamond shone like a silver eye.

"You couldn't help yourself," Ilios said. "You had to keep one."

Malone gritted his teeth as the windmill rotated through a full 360 degrees and kept going. His neck bones cracked and his shoulder screamed as the ropes that bound him dug into his wound. His lungs labored to draw breath. "Stop," he said with voice scarcely more than a whisper.

The windmill ground to a stop. Upside down again, Malone gulped in air against what felt like the weight of his internal organs resting on his lungs. He lamented the loss of the diamond he hadn't known he'd kept. One perfect specimen could have funded his dig for two seasons. No groveling for grants, no holding out his hand like a beggar after a few coins. Someday he wouldn't have to grovel—not for respect, or approval, or peace of mind.

"I thought I emptied all the diamonds out of my pockets," Malone said.

"Ding, not good enough. You meant to steal our diamonds because you're a greedy *duine*."

If Ilios were to be trusted—a big if—he'd found, not planted, the diamond inside Malone's pocket. Malone had a sinking feeling that this was a game with no rules he could beat.

Ilios picked something out if his teeth and called out, "Your question! Make it good."

Chapter Fourteen

Malone had two questions left since he'd squandered one of them. At this point, all he wanted was to return to the top world alive. Not just alive, but with his mind intact. However, a question such as, "How do I survive the other world?" would no doubt lead to a useless answer such as, "By finding the Four Wands."

The windmill began its rotation again. Malone's mind froze, and his body tightened up in response to the torment to come. The ropes groaned and pulled and pushed against his body. He clenched his toes to prevent himself from blacking out.

"I have a question," he said in more of a gurgle than words, but Ilios's acute rabbit ears heard him. The windmill slowed to a halt with Malone in the nine o'clock position. He caught his breath. He didn't have a question; he'd wanted to halt the windmill so he could gather his thoughts.

"One and two and three," Ilios called with what sounded like joy. "Off you go again!"

The windmill jerked. Malone blurted the first question that came to his mind. "What is the perfect question to ask you?"

The gears died back down. Malone struggled to hold his head straight. His neck muscles and tendons felt frayed, but at least he had a moment or two to rest.

"Interesting question." Ilios paced back and forth again, and pretty soon a big smile stretched across his face. "The perfect question to ask me is one I'm doomed to answer false."

Malone frowned. "That's not an answer—that's obvious."

"If you say so. Weren't you listening to me at the beginning?"

Malone's head sagged as his neck muscles started to give out. He racked his mind to remember how Ilios had described the game, but pain drowned out his thoughts.

The windmill's cogs squealed and Malone swung up and back down again. The machinery stopped when Malone reached an upright position. Every cell in his body sent up a murmur of relief.

"Can't have you passing out on me," Ilios said. "Not when we're having such fun."

"Wait a second." Malone attempted a smile. "You used up one of your questions."

Ilios frowned. "I did not."

"You did. When you asked if I weren't listening to you at the beginning."

Ilios's eyes bulged and purple mottling rose on his face. He stomped the ground. "Bloody fecking cheeky gobshite of a *duine*! You confused me with your accusation that my answer was too obvious. And why shouldn't it be when the rules are obvious?"

"The rules are not obvious," Malone said.

"They are!" The pooka stomped his foot again. The froggy mottling grew darker. Spittle flew out of his mouth. "I know what the rules are! Typical nasty *duine* to ruin everything!"

The gears squealed, and the windmill rotated faster than previously. Malone shut his eyes against the twirling horizon line. The windmill squealed in protest, and a board cracked near the central shaft. Malone slipped until the ropes that bound him caught again. The windmill slowed and stopped so he hung upside down. Blood rushed to Malone's head, and he gasped. "We each have one more question."

"I'm next!" Ilios called.

Malone didn't bother protesting that it was his turn to ask the question. It didn't matter, because the so-called rules of this game confused him anyhow. He'd answered his first question falsely, and Ilios had answered his truthfully, yet either one of them could still win.

The mottling on Ilios's face and neck faded. He smiled. "Answer well, *duine*. When was your first act of betrayal?"

The blades started to rotate again, slower, but the movement was enough to distract Malone. His shoulder flared with every wobbly jerk of the blade. In a life full of betrayals, which was the first? Lonan, Anghus's son, flashed through his mind and he forced the memories away. Not pertinent to this torture session. During his life, he'd cheated on exams to achieve the top grades, he'd lied about his qualifications to land jobs, and so much more—none of which counted as betrayals. Betrayals were more personal and treacherous.

"As revenge against my dad when I was eight, I told a lie about him—that he'd poached on the big family's land. They beat the shite out of him as punishment."

Ilios's triumphant grin faded. Malone smiled for the first time since the game started. A moment later, Malone's confusion returned.

"Wrong!" Ilios said. "How could you have lied again? You're smarter than you look, *duine*, but we're not done yet."

"I told you the truth," Malone said.

"Liar!" Ilios yelled. "You can't help yourself. You were always a greedy gobshite. You're telling me you don't remember pushing your younger sister Maggie off the swing so you could have it for yourself? Huh? Your sister, who ended up with a concussion and a scar on her forehead because of you? That was your first betrayal!"

"I revealed the earliest betrayal that I remember."

"Impossible! I remember my life back to the womb!"

"It's not like that for humans," Malone said.

"It's not?" Ilios considered him, disappointment evident in his droopy ears. "You *duine* are a strange lot." He began pacing again, with head bowed, fingering his lips. "Never mind. A tie goes to me for the win!"

A tie? And how would that be possible?

The windmill halted with Malone in an upright position. Understanding started to glimmer. Malone had provided two false answers. Apparently, telling the truth was beside the point, which shouldn't surprise him because this was a pooka he was dealing with. Ilios had tricked him into believing they were supposed to tell the truth, but the goal was consistency, whether falsehoods or truths. In which case, yes, a tie was possible. Bloody pooka.

Malone recalled Ilios's answer to his first question. Question: What is the perfect question to ask you? Answer: The perfect question to ask me is one I'm doomed to answer false. Now Ilios's seemingly obvious and useless answer made sense. Since Ilios had answered his first question honestly, Malone must now ask him something that he couldn't help but answer dishonestly.

Malone crossed his fingers and prayed his sense of the pooka was correct. "Here's my question. When's the last time you broke a rule?"

Ilios raised his arms as if saluting a nonexistent sun. His smile turned beatific as he dropped his arms again. "That, my nasty *duine*, is easy to answer, because I'm on probation. Last week I snuck to the top world to gallop through the waves. I got caught." He shrugged. "First time for everything. It will be a while before I pull that stunt again."

Malone pressed his crossed fingers tighter. He croaked rather than shouted with triumph. "Wrong!"

Moddey had been sitting quietly throughout the game. Now he circled the grumbling pooka, poking him with his nose.

"You broke the rules of this very game by not answering my first question," Malone said. "I asked 'what, why?' about having to answer three questions. You never responded, which means you answered my first question with the truth, and the second one not. Inconsistency loses, so you lose."

Ilios sucked in his lips with a hiss. His face contorted with rage. The blue light swirled around him and a moment later he leapt out of it with furious equine squeals and gleaming hooves striking out at Malone. Ilios reared above him with eyes as bright as two suns and smoke billowing from his nostrils. The wheel of fortune rocked with each strike from Ilios's hooves. The wooden blades squealed and from within the mill house gears groaned. With a crack, one of the blades broke away from the rotor hub and crashed to the ground. The windmill rocked and more boards rained down around Malone. He pressed himself against the blade he was bound to but too late. A piece of wood crashed into his head and the world went dark.

CHAPTER FIFTEEN

Malone's first thought as consciousness revealed itself in aching waves was "shrapnel." He must have stepped on a landmine or stood too close to one. He struggled to move under the weight of an inert, war-torn corpse. His muscles screamed with the effort.

He opened his eyes to a blood-red sky. Worse than a battlefield—he was in hell. No, worse than hell: the other world. He shifted his head to see a giant dog-wolf nose and a pair of fiery eyes staring at him. Beyond Moddey, the annihilated remnants of the windmill lay strewn around them. Malone was thankful for one small mercy: the pooka had disappeared.

The windmill blade pressed him into the ground. Unbidden, tears seeped from his eyes. He wasn't sure he had the fortitude to manage the pain anymore. He thought of Ilios's stream where he'd floated, liberated from himself and the pain of being himself for a few moments.

Moddey poked his forehead and then began gnawing on the rope that bound Malone to the blade. The rope had partially shredded under Ilios's onslaught so it didn't take long for Moddey to chew through the fibers.

"Leave me alone," Malone said.

Moddey poked him harder this time. He pulled at the rope to loosen it from around Malone's body. Blinking away tears, Malone counted down three, two, one. On a heave, he managed to shift an inch that felt like plummeting off a cliff. He closed his eyes. He let himself sink into sweet darkness, knowing that when Moddey wasn't mauling him, his orders included watching over him. Malone would be safe enough for now.

The next time he woke up, Moddey gripped his good arm. His ears twitched in response to uneven breaths of air, the rumble of them like far-off waves, as he yanked Malone out from under the detritus. A low wheeze shook the ground under Malone's head. Moddey whined and pulled harder. Moddey wasn't immune to this place, after all.

The bog man. Jesus, Malone had forgotten about Danu's mummified son.

A vision of the creature's shining, black eyes within sunken hollows, its slow blinks as it adjusted to sight again, the swivel of its head before it raised itself to stand for the first time in hundreds, thousands, who knew how many, generations galvanized Malone despite the agony that nearly blacked him out again. He managed to crawl the rest of the way out from under the wreckage with his weight on one arm. The smell of blood coated his mouth. He touched his head and discovered a swollen gash.

With excruciating slowness, he removed his jacket, sweater, and undershirt. He used a rusted nail to help him tear the undershirt into strips that he tied around his shoulder. Next, he forced the sweater into Moddey's mouth and pulled until the wool ripped. Malone used the sweater to bind his arm against his chest to immobilize the shoulder.

"Oh god," he sighed.

Even that small alleviation of his pain was a vast improvement. Shaking with the effort not to keel over, he pulled the jacket onto one arm and over both shoulders, and tucked the empty sleeve into the sweater. He wobbled as he stood and braced himself against his furry minder.

"Now what's my next move?" Malone said.

A silver glow emanated from beneath a pile of wood and gears where the windmill had fallen in on itself. Malone lurched forward. The Sword of Light. Had to be.

He cleared broken boards and rusted cogs and wheels out of the way. The hilt of the sword with its Ogham letters for "light" appeared. Malone reached out and the moment he touched the hilt a wave of wellbeing coursed through him. The pain receded enough for him to function. He paused to rest and check Moddey's eyes. He might be imagining it, but he could swear their yellow glow had also receded. Hopefully winning the challenge against Ilios had earned him a temporary reprieve.

"What about the second wand? That bastard pooka said he would reveal it to me."

He glanced around the wreckage. A warm glow still emanated from within the gap where he'd found the sword. He hadn't noticed this light previously because the sword's luminosity drowned it out. He thought he knew which Tuatha Dé Danaan treasure it represented, and if he was correct, he couldn't carry it away with him.

With that in mind, instead of clearing more wreckage, he pulled off his boots and socks and sat with legs outstretched in front of him. With his good arm he scooted himself feet first into the gap between broken windmill boards and toward the light source. Warmth reached out to welcome him. He hesitated. This could be another trick, but then he caught sight of Moddey's twitching ears and remembered the bog man. The reverberation of the bog man's breath no longer rumbled below ground; it now had substance, a rhythm of inhalation and exhalation.

He scooted the last few inches toward the glow. His foot brushed warm stone, and a roar of joy greeted him. Malone's heart soared. His awe was so profound he froze for a moment before stroking the ancient stone that had been hidden within the wheel of fortune all along. The stone reacted to his touch with an ecstatic sigh.

"Hear that, Moddey? The Stone of Destiny accepts me."

He pressed in with his feet, and the mythological coronation stone of kings sang out in the jubilant tone it reserved for rightful kings or queens. Rightful heirs.

Malone grinned as he pulled himself out of the gap. The stone's restorative power surged into his shoulder and the rest of his broken body. The Stone of Destiny ensured a long reign, which could mean that he wouldn't die down here. He had a destiny to fulfill.

Destiny, not fate as Danu had said. The Ogham puzzle, *heir's death*, flitted through his thoughts, but he set the message aside in favor of focusing on what the Stone of Destiny seemed to indicate. Maybe he was on his way to becoming a king in this other world, or better yet, in the top world.

He tested his arm and found that as long as he held it close to his body, the pain remained steady at a dull throb. He slipped on his shoes and socks. The far-off whoosh of the bog man's breath came from no direction and all directions at once. Malone grabbed a wooden board from one of the windmill blades. Hardly Danu's staff, but it would suffice. Leaning against Moddey, he used the board to stand. He wobbled with lightheadedness and willed himself to retain the doses of healing the sword and stone had provided. For magical implements, they weren't all that effective, but maybe that was the game Danu played with him. Keep him alive long enough to reach the final torture.

"Which way now, Moddey old boy?" Wait, if he was a king—of sorts—then he had the right to demand help. He cleared his throat and called up to the sky that wasn't a sky. "Take me to the next wand challenge."

He waited.

"I command you to take me to the next wand challenge."

The breeze with no temperature or scent bent the fleshy grass. Thankfully, the bastard faery twinkles weren't swarming him in an attempt to move him along. His instinct told him to head in the opposite direction of the bog man. Unfortunately, he couldn't tell which direction that was.

"'Allo!" he called. "Aren't you supposed to obey me now?"

"I'll obey you," a voice said.

A vice-like grip snaked around his neck and pulled him backwards.

Chapter Sixteen

"Abhartach," Malone said.

Another arm entwined itself around his torso and held him tight, almost lovingly. A tip of tongue caressed his neck, and Malone trembled with emotions at odds between disgust and arousal. He sensed rather than heard Abhartach absorbing his scent, but he dared not move in case the blood drinker decided to sink his teeth into his neck.

Abhartach's voice brushed Malone's ear with a sweet scent that reminded him of death just this side of rotting. "The Stone of Destiny accepted you, but you may not like for what."

Abhartach's hands continued roving over Malone's body, and his voice continued whispering into Malone's ear. "Lucky for you the stone favored you, or else I'd have devoured you already."

"And not left the pleasure of killing me for Danu's bog child? For shame."

Abhartach's profile entered Malone's peripheral vision. His cheek rubbed against Malone's. "Don't talk to me about shame."

Malone glanced down to see the rope that bound Abhartach's feet trailing away from him and disappearing up into the sky that was not a sky. "Why aren't you hanging?" he said.

In answer, Abhartach's jagged nails dug into Malone, and with strength that belied his stringy appearance, he hefted Malone up. With a jerk, the rope upended them so they hung upside down. The ground reversed away as they shot up into the air. The decimated windmill shrank to a speck and the curve of whatever planet-like place this was became apparent.

Abhartach unwrapped one of his arms from around Malone's body. Graceful fingers danced in front of Malone's face before they flung images up in the air like cards. Malone grabbed the closest one. He caught sight of a moon before the image dissolved.

Abhartach's laugh burrowed into Malone's psyche, an anticipatory glee that sent shivers down his spine. "You're sure to have fun now."

The sensation of being pulled by a cosmic string continued until Abhartach flung Malone into the void. A moment later, the ground greeted him squarely against his bad shoulder. Pain engulfed him in a white, hot blaze, and he may have screamed, may have blacked out, before becoming aware of the roar of an incoming tide. After the preternatural quietude of the fleshy grass plain, the grumble and slosh of waves rolling in on a coastline filled Malone with a ghost of comfort.

He'd survived.

For now.

He rolled off his injured shoulder and inhaled the familiar scents of algae and rotting mollusks and sea salt. He let the moment of respite sink into his aching bones. His shoulder felt detached from his body, but he welcomed the pain over the strange effect that Abhartach had on him.

He'd landed in a beach cove surrounded by soaring cliffs. The moon's silvery glow shimmered against lavender whitecaps and a deep purple sea. The reddish hue he'd grown used to no longer saturated the air, which was darker now, like raw amethyst crystals—rich, cool, and sparkling.

Padding steps approached. Moonlight caught the fire within Moddey's eyes as he perched next to Malone. The tide eddied around his feet, oddly temperature-less like the breeze on the fleshy plain. He'd lost the shirt and sweater he'd used to bind his shoulder, along with his jacket. Sea spray misted his skin. In the silvery purple night, his torso shone smooth as alabaster, like a living statue, and for a moment, he wondered if he was already dead.

He examined the swollen and bloodied joint that used to be a functional shoulder. The joke could be that he'd died and this was his hell. But no, his shoulder told him he was alive enough. Misshapen and swollen now, livid with bruises, and puffy red around the edges of the wound. He grimaced at the grind of bone ends rubbing against each other when he sat up. The rejuvenating effect of the Stone of Destiny was already wearing off. In its place, the first creeping tendrils of infection and fever wormed their ways through his body.

He picked up the sword and grabbed onto Moddey's ruff to haul himself to his feet. The effort broke him out in a sweat. His vision wavered and he swallowed down nausea.

Abhartach had warned him that he may not like what the stone's acceptance meant. In other words, his delusions of grandeur didn't amount to a piss in the wind. He wasn't a king; he was barely an archaeologist. On the bright side, only two more wands to go until he earned his freedom.

He leaned against Moddey, eye to eye now, and scanned the secluded cove. At low tide, he might be able to skirt the cliffs, but for now he was trapped. A fog of sea spray enveloped him as he hobbled up the beach toward the cliffs in search of cover. Aside from the tide, nothing moved. The cliffs towered above him and blocked out half the sky. He placed a hand on the cool surface. Dozens of sparkles shot toward him from deeper within the cliff face.

He lifted his hand. The sparkles died back. When he stroked the cliff side again, they shot toward him. Their tingling sensation felt like of pins and needles. He lifted his hand away and continued on in search of an entrance into the cliffs. With each step, his exhaustion worsened.

Malone longed to invite Moddey to bite off his shoulder. He'd lose an arm in the process, but he was willing to pay that price. He couldn't remember when he'd last eaten. Time eluded him, and the tide continued rising.

He leaned against the cliff face and slid down so that he sat facing the water. The tingling crystal surface against his back soothed him. A pleasant inertia stole over him. Death might not be so bad in front of this view of a vast water like liquid amethysts. His eyes drifted shut. When he opened them again, a pair of liquid brown eyes surrounded by a thick fringe of eyelashes blinked back at him. He wrapped his arms around himself, felt goose bumps and sweat. His teeth chattered.

"Is that real?" he asked Moddey.

In answer, Moddey licked the seal in welcome, and it acknowledged the dog-wolf with a soft grunt. The seal turned aside and waded through the shallows toward the other end of the cove. With perked ears, Moddey followed. Malone knew what perked ears meant. Pay attention. With a moan, he dragged his body up to standing. He stumbled and caught himself. The seal waddled out of the water and up a slope toward the entrance of a smaller cove. A blue shimmer swirled around it.

Pooka. Trying to trick him with a doe-like gaze. Malone wiped sweat out of his eyes and in doing so, missed the moment of transformation. He caught his breath at the sight of a naked woman bathed in moonlight. Wavy brown hair hung to her waist. She beckoned him and entered the smaller cove.

Malone managed to steady himself enough to follow the woman. He paused when he reached a pelt of seal skin. Ah, a selkie.

Her voice sang of the deeps when she said, "Please don't touch."

Moddey growled, and Malone obeyed. Rule noted. Do not mess about with a selkie skin.

She waited as he approached her one excruciating step at a time. His legs quivered with the effort. He grabbed on to Moddey again.

"I'm here to guide you," she said. "Ilios wasn't supposed to almost kill you, but then you weren't supposed to poison his stream with your humanity. You are a surprise."

"A good thing, I hope."

The selkie stood before him, pristine and beautiful in the purple-glazed night. Malone drank in the sight of her. The selkie's intelligence and for lack of a better word, "humanity," shone out of her eyes.

"Many of us are disturbed that you would find the pooka stream pleasurable," she said. "We call it the Yearning Stream because Ilios uses the water to nurse his grievances."

"What does that mean?"

"What you think you yearn for gleams as false as your reflecting pasture. However, beneath the surface there might be a forgotten part of yourself that's worth saving. Time will tell." The selkie continued walking. "Come along and avoid the cliff face. It weaves a strange spell on top worlders. You'd have lingered in a tranced state until you drowned."

"What about Caorthannach? Will the bog man find me here?"

The selkie paused, confusion evident in the slant of her head. "Bog man?"

"Danu's son—the reason I landed here in the first place."

"Ah." Her smile turned pitying. "You are confused, but you'll learn the truth of it soon enough." She closed her eyes and leaned her head back. "Danu's son follows your path through the other world. Come now."

He followed her to an opening in the cliff. "You can shelter in there," the selkie said, and reversed course back to the water. Her eagerness to inhabit her selkie skin was evident as she ran across the sand. Graceful limbs blurred into a dance of lights and then her seal form dove into the waves.

Moddey barked a goodbye and followed Malone as he ducked into the opening. By now, exhaustion and pain had carved out his core. He leaned against the rock wall and held up the sword to illuminate a tunnel. The luminescence within the cliff walls was muted here and the sound of the tide receded as he walked deeper into the cliff side.

He wondered what story Anghus had concocted to explain his disappearance and that of the bog man artifact. Maybe the rest of the locals assumed Malone had smuggled the artifact off the Isle of Man—which wouldn't be beneath him anyhow. He remembered Ilios's accusation that he'd pushed Maggie off the swing so he could have it for himself. The misdeed had the ring of truth.

The tunnel narrowed until he stood before a narrow seam in the rock. He squeezed through it into a cavern the size of a cathedral. Behind him, Moddey whined but managed to fit through the opening also. Hundreds of Malone's flickering faery nemeses floated above them and lit up the vast space. A dull thud like distant thunder caused Moddey's ears to twitch.

Two Tuatha Dé Danaan treasures remained: the Dagda's Cauldron and the Spear of Lugh. Unfortunately, he was too tired and thirsty to ponder the horrors of the next challenge or how finding the treasures might help him escape this dung hole. The sand underfoot looked as soft as a blanket and invited him to lie down much as the pooka's stream had invited him to float.

His thoughts drifted, his vision swam, he floated in fever. He sank his feet into the sand and wished it were a stream that would cool fever and warm away chills at the same time. The thing to do would be to coat himself in a sand blanket. Like a water blanket. Soft. Soothing. Either way, he'd float well enough.

Moddey ignored him, sniffing ahead with a vague tail wag. His benign behavior signaled permission enough for Malone. He began digging a shallow trench. His fingers grew hazy as if they were melting off his body. Maybe he was about to disperse into a million tiny pieces—boom, like one of his platoon mates—and maybe all the digging and submerging he got up to in the other world had meaning.

No, that made zero sense because he'd managed to hurdle through the air, too. Even so, he sensed that he was sinking deeper and deeper into this place. Or, more likely, that the other world was digging its tendrils deeper into him.

"What does it matter?" he murmured.

As he dug, he rubbed the sand over his skin. Unlike the dirt at the dolmen, the sand clung to him like a second, warm skin—like a selkie skin, he imagined—and soon enough he crawled into the shallow trench and swept more dirt over himself in a snug cocoon. This strange and terrifying world slipped away and he sank into sleep.

CHAPTER SEVENTEEN

Malone floated in dreams of pork and potato stew thickened with whole milk straight from the cow, and soda bread fresh from the oven covered with a thick layer of butter. Most of all, he dreamed of water flowing over his tongue and down his throat to quench his almighty thirst. Voices murmured around him, the comforting hum of women talking amongst themselves. His mother and aunties at their Sunday meal preparations while he loitered underfoot, every now and then earning a swat for his efforts.

"It's the delirium," one voice said.

Malone shifted within his warm cocoon of sleep.

"True, but it's still odd," said a second woman. "The same thing happened at the dolmen."

A grunt and then a third woman retorted, "Because he's too flawed. We knew this."

Malone drifted toward unwilling consciousness. He recognized two of the voices and understood who the third woman must be. The Morrigan, the three goddess sisters of war. He'd met Nemain and Macha. The snarly third one must be Badb, the harbinger of doom.

He slitted his eyes open to check his surroundings. The cavern now pulled double duty as a gathering place with silken pillows covering the ground and a crackling fire warming his back. Hundreds of candles created a warm glow, and here and there, the vague outlines of faery beings draped themselves over the pillows. More lights danced through the air in time to a melodic flute song. The Morrigan relaxed with heads bent to their work as they polished and repaired a collection of spears, blades, and armor. Nemain, the fairest, with a tender heart toward Moddey Dhoo; Macha with her darker features and sapphire eyes; and last, Badb, angular and stark, with pure white skin and pure black hair.

He'd entered a womb-like place—a female place—and rather than comfort, his anxiety spiked. Here were mysteries he would never comprehend. Abhartach with his floating images had revealed the moon, symbol of the female. None of this was random. Abhartach had sent him to their den.

His stomach grumbled, and the Morrigan went silent. Malone clamped his jaw tight to prevent his teeth from chattering with the force of the fever that raged inside him. He shifted but found he couldn't move. His sand blanket had transformed itself into a hard shell. As soon as he realized he was trapped, his skin began to itch, his muscles cried out to be stretched and his shoulder throbbed against the chrysalis-like casing.

Nemain started toward him, but Macha held her arm out to block her. With a head shake, she said, "I warned him, but he refused to listen."

Malone's voice came out a croak. "Warned me about what?"

Badb's contemptuous frown almost flayed him. "You're encased in your own folly. Again. Look at you. I've never met a human so colossally stupid."

"In other words," Macha said, "delusions rule you. You trap yourself in them so that the truth eludes you."

"What truth would that be?"

Badb snorted. "He's not fit, I tell you."

Malone struggled against his confinement, but the harder he pushed, the more the sand cocoon clung to him. His destroyed shoulder sent teeth-rattling waves of pain through his body. White lights swam before his eyes. He gave up and gave in to the chills. He'd drink his own sweat if his body carried enough moisture to produce any.

Unconsciousness weaved its deadening way into his thoughts. He bit his tongue to remain awake—to focus— and tasted blood. Beyond the flute song, fire's hiss, and clank of the Morrigan's weapons, Malone caught another sound: the thud of the bog man's footsteps.

His tongue stuck to the roof of his mouth when he swallowed. "Don't you hear it? I command you to free me."

Badb straightened and whipped toward him so fast Malone didn't have time to blink before she held his face between her clawed hands. Her touch seared his skin. Behind her, Moddey Dhoo crouched with eyes glowing and teeth bared.

Badb's eyes swirled black within black. "You speak to us like that again, and we shall rip out your heart through your throat and feed it to Moddey."

Macha pulled Badb away. "Enough, sister. That's not our call."

"It's the fever talking," Nemain said.

"Sod you all," Malone said.

The glow within Moddey's eyes grew and the ruff around his neck thickened. The last remnants of dog dissolved into wolf, but Malone couldn't care less. Let them maul him or kill him or send him to the hell they thought he deserved. Anything would be better than this exquisite pain that had no outlet except through words. So that's what he did. He hurled insults at them through parched vocal cords with no clear idea of what he was saying. Fever and infection had entered his brain, but he didn't care about that either.

Moddey Dhoo sprang toward him. Spent, Malone lifted his head to expose his neck. "Go on then. Do it. I dare you."

Chapter Eighteen

Saliva dripped from Moddey's jaws as he adjusted his grip on Malone's neck without breaking the skin.

"Moddey, no." A fourth woman spoke from behind Malone. Her voice drifted out of her old as the moon in the sky. "Release him."

With a whine, Moddey opened his jaws and stepped back. His fiery gaze remained fixed on Malone. The Morrigan shimmered in blue light and then rose up as ravens with strident cawing. They circled above Malone's head before retreating into the glimmering heights of the cavern.

"Moddey, if you would, please," the woman said.

Malone tensed as the wolf approached him again, but rather than attack him, he shoved his muzzle under the cocoon that encased Malone and heaved him over so that he faced the opposite direction. Before him stood a crone with long silver hair and soft skin etched with time. Her large eyes reminded him of the selkie's: deep brown and all-knowing. She wore a simple shift in shimmering white. The heavenly smell that had set Malone's stomach to growling emanated from her bronze cauldron. She sprinkled a plant that resembled moss into her brew and stirred.

"The Dagda's Cauldron," he whispered.

The third wand. The cauldron of Dagda, god of fertility and wisdom, which was said to provide an endless supply of food and drink. No one left unsatisfied from the Dagda's Cauldron.

"No," the old woman said. "This is my cauldron, called Awen. You must pass its test to be deemed worthy of replenishing yourself from the Dagda's Cauldron."

The bog man's footsteps grew louder. The old woman appeared unperturbed as she continued. "You are dying. Blood poison."

Badb's voice floated from within the dance of faeries. "We die as we live. This one was always polluted."

"Possibly," the crone said in a placid way before addressing Malone again. "However, the blood poison is not your concern at the moment."

"Who are you?" Malone said.

"I'm Cerridwen."

Malone's thoughts stuttered weak and ill-formed—he was nothing but a ball of hot and cold and thirst and hunger and pain—but he recalled his mother's stories about Cerridwen, the ancient enchantress often called the Hag of Creation.

"Awen's test," he said. "Tell me what I must do."

She waved her hand and the Sword of Light materialized on the ground beside him. "All submit to the will of the sword."

"I know the lore," Malone said.

She shook her head with a *tsk*. "But did *you* submit to the sword as the questing beast instructed? I suppose you weren't paying attention. Typical of the men of your world." She leaned over to sniff the steam rising out of her cauldron. "Would be easier on you now if you had submitted then. Now you must submit my way."

"I have submitted. Look at me."

Badb's caw mocked him. "He's not fit!"

A thud echoed through the cavern. Too close.

"You can't wield the Sword of Light unless you submit first," Cerridwen said. "You're running out of time."

Malone remembered how the sword froze up on him when he attempted to use it against Moddey, but for the ebbing life of him, he had no clue what she meant. The will of the sword remained unknown to him, and he refused to commune with it while Caorthannach's fire-spitting, bog-blackened self approached. In his delirium, he fancied the bog man's breaths already mingled with the breezes on the beach.

Cerridwen lifted her ladle and sipped the soup. Malone's mouth watered. He wept with frustration and a longing he couldn't define. "I don't know what I'm doing," he said.

The crone stopped her ministrations to study him. A smile crinkled the skin around her eyes and mouth. "Why do you suppose you're here?" she said.

"For chopping the sacred hawthorn and for releasing the bog man."

She stirred her concoction and sipped again, this time crinkling her nose. "Perfect." She addressed him again. "True enough. Insult to injury."

Cerridwen spoke in riddles like the others. Insult to what injury? He drifted away again, then roused himself at the word "blame."

"—and the responsibility shall be yours," Cerridwen was saying. "If you're lucky, or not, depending on how you look at it." She considered him. "Do you truly wish for death? We can grant you that wish easily enough."

He wasn't sure. He was broken in ways far worse than his shoulder. The other world had ripped him open, but apparently that was not enough.

He recalled his belief in Lonan's barmy tale about a giant bog body thousands of years old. How the dream—or maybe obsession—of such a discovery had spurred him toward survival after they found themselves trapped behind enemy lines and forced to abandon the dugout. The two of them had hobbled on diseased feet toward the closest decimated shell of a village. Malone as the senior man found them shelter inside a barn. They huddled under clothing that they tore off corpses and rifled through pockets for bits of preserved meat or biscuit, with only Lonan's tale to keep them company. Malone had found himself latching onto the idea of the bog man. Since the war, he'd labored to heal, to raise money, to educate himself—all to uncover the bog body and make his name. To what purpose he no longer knew.

Cerridwen ladled a portion of soup into a ceramic bowl and stepped around her cauldron. Her tunic shimmered with golden reflections from the flames. She stooped in front of him and tilted the bowl toward his mouth. Malone gulped the pungent broth. Cerridwen pulled the bowl away. "That's enough to start."

The warm slide of broth over his tongue woke him up again. His body screamed for more. Cerridwen settled herself beside him on one of the pillows, watching. Waiting. A prick of disquiet scuttled up Malone's spine. A second later, an electrical storm ripped through his body. Thousands of tiny hammers pounded his nerve endings and convulsions threw him against the sides of the cocoon.

Chapter Nineteen

After several minutes, the convulsions receded to spasms, and that's when Malone let loose his screams. The fresh onslaught had turned his shoulder into a molten lava pool of unremitting agony. Yes, he thought, I could die now.

"You poisoned me," he said.

Cerridwen grabbed a chunk of Malone's hair and lifted his head. Whatever she saw in his gaze made her drop his head again. "The brew finds the poison within you, that is all."

The spasms subsided to stomach cramps. This was the next wand test then; he must survive Cerridwen's cauldron. He must submit, as she'd said, but to what? He couldn't think straight. The blood poison—in other words, sepsis—corroded him from the inside out.

"Awen fosters inspiration and transformation," she said. "Transformation can give rise to inspiration, but transformation is not easy."

Malone pressed his lips together. With strength that belied her withered limbs, she yanked his head back so fast he gasped, and she poured another mouthful of the liquid into his mouth. She held his jaw shut until he swallowed. Another conflagration ignited him. His screams echoed off the cavern walls. The flute music faded out, and the beings draped on the pillows shrank to sparkles and dispersed.

He thought he heard the voice of Nemain, the kind one. "He'll not survive."

"He may not, that is true," Cerridwen said. "Yet, I sense glimmers."

"OK," he whispered when the convulsions subsided again. "I'll submit. You win."

Cerridwen's wizened face appeared in front of him. "This isn't about me. This is about you. Your torment will worsen until you either understand at long last, or you die. The choice is yours."

Malone drifted on waves of pain and memory. He pictured himself dodging incoming fire, stretching toward his vast future. Escaping and surviving. He did what it took whether it meant surviving his childhood or surviving the war. He'd refused to submit to anything after that fateful day under the May tree when he'd cried his eyes out and vowed never to show weakness again.

Yet, here he lay, weak as the boy he once was. Perhaps Cerridwen was trying to tell him to embrace his weakness. If so, then the witch had won, full stop.

Cerridwen jerked his head back again. He shut his eyes to contain tears of mortal fear, but they arrived unbidden. I am submitting, he repeated to himself. I am. IamIamIam.

"No, you aren't. At all. You must be strong."

A raven's shriek echoed from the upper reaches of the cavern. One of the Morrigan sisters flew toward Malone, and one swirl of blue later Badb landed on her feet next to Cerridwen. She grabbed for the bowl.

"Enough of this. This one isn't worthy."

She pushed Cerridwen out of the way and straddled Malone. With one hand pressed against his forehead, she lowered the bowl to his clenched lips. An endless stream of Cerridwen's brew flowed over his mouth and nostrils. More ravens cawed and landed next to Malone. Nemain and Macha appeared.

"Stop," Macha grabbed Badb's arm, but Badb pushed her away.

Malone's lungs heaved and he inhaled the liquid through his nose. The sting of it made him cough, and the moment he did, the brew filled his mouth. Badb's shadow grew over him. Firelight lit her up like the war wraith she was, and her voice boomed like detonated landmines.

"Swallow!"

Malone sputtered and spit against Cerridwen's poison. The fluid entered his lungs with each heaving breath and cough.

Nemain's and Macha's voices rose, and over them, another sound. THUD. Danu's son honed in on him, well past the Wheel of Fortune and the Stone of Destiny, covering distances that Malone didn't know he'd traveled.

Darkness crept into Malone's vision. His mind drifted away from the Morrigan. In those last life-draining moments he saw not fire and war and treachery but the May tree once again. Its froth of fragrant flowers floated around him through a haze of tears. A small moment in his life—the way this father had shamed him that day—but he'd held on to the memory like a toxic talisman. Humiliation at the hands of his father wasn't a novelty, but that day he had to subjugate himself to his father's will while the village watched. His father took great pleasure in yelling at Malone to dance until his feet fell off. Long after the girls wandered off, he alone circled the May tree surrounded by pitying looks while his father continued hounding him, his friends at his side, all of them drunk and gleeful in their cruelty.

No one, not one adult or friend or even his mother had protected him. He was alone then, as he was now in his dying.

CHAPTER TWENTY

Every atom in Malone's body flared to life at the same time, each one as sensitive as a nerve ending. He wailed in outrage at the sheer shock of life itself as the cocoon that encased him disappeared. His limbs unfurled with a painful grind of joints, leaving him splayed as a newborn babe.

"Shut him up," Badb hissed.

Nemain knelt next to him and implored him to hush. In response, he recoiled into a shivering ball. A resounding boom shook the cavern. And then another. Malone closed his eyes against the image of the bog man pounding on the outside of the cavern, its body a shiny black relief map of every band of muscle and strip of tendon.

The pinkish twinkles of the other crowd vanished. Badb and Macha hunched with Cerridwen near the cauldron.

"I knew it as soon as I saw him," Badb said. "He'd only submit on the brink of death."

Cerridwen's voice vibrated with rage. "That wasn't the brink of death—that was death. You've left him vulnerable."

"What of it?" Badb retorted. "You were taking too long."

Macha interrupted. "That's enough. Let's be done."

"Sit up now," Nemain said to Malone.

His good arm gave out under him when he tried to lift himself. Nemain propped him up. His muscles ached and fever wracked his body. Around them, the cavern shuddered and crackled.

"What happened?" he said.

"Badb lost her patience—as she does—and took you to submission too fast, yet by some miracle you survived. You need to remember."

"I'm fresh out of coherent thoughts at the moment."

Nemain glanced at her sisters and Cerridwen, still haggling. "This isn't about intellect. It's about what you felt as you died. Delusions hide the truth, but death reveals truth's soul."

Nemain pressed her hands against his chest, and his heart surged to meet her touch. "The core of you. You wouldn't have survived Cerridwen's cauldron if it didn't perceive something within you that was worth saving. You must have submitted to something."

Understanding rose to the surface. The boy under the May tree who'd hardened his heart—no more crying allowed—and thereafter used ambition as the scaffold to build his life. In the end, his ambition supported nothing but loneliness so vast he never recognized it for what it was. No wonder he'd attacked the bog man's hawthorn tree with such vengeance. A reminder of his origins.

He nodded, submission complete. He thought he'd squashed out hurt and abandonment and shame—and hope—in favor of the shriveled, furious desire to prove himself to his father, to the whole world. But he remained that lonely boy at heart.

Another boom echoed off the walls of the cavern, and then another. The cavern quaked under the onslaught of the bog man's fists, and the walls crackled and split like ice on a frozen lake. The ghostly lights of the faery beings flickered and scattered.

Cerridwen pushed her way between the sisters and stooped in front of Malone. Her great brown eyes peered into his soul. Her skin soft and downy and crinkled—a wizened and beautiful face, Malone thought, in his delirium.

"Come," Cerridwen said to the Morrigan. "Help me with him."

The women hauled Malone to his feet as all good soldiers could do and dragged him toward the cauldron. A monstrous, blackened fist blasted through the wall and the cavern came alive with sparks of flying rock. The bog man stretched its arm into the hole it had created. The peat-soaked, ancient flesh now lean and muscular rather than withered through mummification.

Badb voiced her objections again. "He's not worthy. He has yet to understand why he's here."

"Enough!" Cerridwen ordered. "He's worthy of the Dagda's Cauldron. The rest remains to be seen."

Above them, the bog man withdrew its arm. The wind that was the bog man's breath roared as if from a thousand coal furnaces, blackened and foul, and snuffed out the candles, leaving them with the glow from the cauldron fire. Its fist crashed through the wall again. More rock shattered around them. Malone flinched away from the shards that struck his skin. He floated out of his body, away from this misery to the May tree with its snowfall of petals. A small hand within his own, and a body leaning against his. "You were very brave to dance with us," Maggie, his loyal wee sister with the scar on her forehead, said. "Most boys would have taken the belt instead."

A kiss on his cheek before she held a May branch in front of him. "Make a wish and blow," she said, "and your wish will come true."

"I'll show him," Malone had whispered just before he yelled at Maggie to leave him the fecking hell alone. The moment he betrayed himself. The moment he stopped crying.

Nemain pinched his cheek. "Malone, get back here."

A gleaming golden cauldron four feet high and four feet in diameter stood in place of Cerridwen's bronze cauldron. Within it, a thick soup burbled its invitation. A shard-like rain fell around them and black smoke swirled above their heads. The bog man's fist crashed through the cavern wall again.

"Drink," Cerridwen ordered.

Malone's stomach cramped with both hunger and sickness, yet a scent like fresh honey and warm bread almost made him swoon. The moment his lips touched the cauldron's bounty, instinct took over despite his swollen tongue and cramps. He slurped up the liquid and moaned with pleasure at a taste like pure light and perfect nourishment, like the satisfaction after a hearty meal, like satiation and wellbeing. He drank until his stomach could take no more and he slid down the side of the cauldron in a daze.

"What's wrong with him?" Nemain said.

Cerridwen lifted his head. "The Dagda's Cauldron judges this one partially worthy, so he's only partially healed."

Malone's mouth worked to form words that came out muddy and unformed. "Where's Moddey? I want Moddey Dhoo."

"Hmm." Cerridwen studied him as if with fresh eyes. "You feel connected to him. Just as it should be."

The wolf approached with ruff as thick as a lion's mane and fiery eyes like lanterns. Here stood the one being in this cursed other world that behaved with unequivocal honesty. No riddles in his behavior, only acceptance or condemnation. Malone trusted Moddey.

Another rending crash shook them. Moddey's ears flattened, and his mournful howls filled the cavern. Malone pulled himself up to standing inch by excruciating inch. Panting, he leaned against the cauldron to stabilize himself. His injured arm no longer hung limply at his side. He raised his hand and clutched the rim of the cauldron. Pain radiated from his shoulder, but the fact that he had enough strength to clutch his hand gave him hope that his body would mend itself. Eventually.

He continued bracing himself against the cauldron as the bog man's second fist crashed through the wall. A chunk of rock the size of Malone's head landed beside him.

"Our part is done," Cerridwen said. "Come away."

Nemain handed Malone the Sword of Light. "Remember this. You'll need it."

The Morrigan and Cerridwen swirled away on purple pinpricks of light, leaving Malone alone.

CHAPTER TWENTY-ONE

The cavern crackled under the bog man's onslaught. Flying crystal shards glinted in the firelight. Malone reached out for Moddey and entwined his free hand in the wolf's fur. Together, they stumbled toward the entrance to the passageway that led to the cove.

The bog man's breath filled the cavern and swirled on breezes that whistled through the holes in the walls. The groan of unused vocal cords sang of the earth's primordial past, of colliding land masses and volcano eruptions. The sound sent shockwaves through the earth, the beginnings of language in those sounds.

The shadow of the bog man's vast arms filtered through the smoke and falling debris. They unfurled like blackened tentacles above Malone and the wolf. Cracks in the cavern branched out like a million shattering mirrors. Malone willed himself not to drop into a protective crouch in reaction to the rending snap of the cavern walls. His lungs caught on shallow inhalations. His fingers went numb and his vision wavered as adrenalin and war terrors surged through him.

Whining, Moddey dragged Malone forward and pushed him into the tunnel that led back to the cove. He nosed in after Malone, but the aperture now proved too narrow for him. He yelped as the rock cut into his shoulders and pawed at the aperture, panting in terror.

"You can do it," Malone said.

Malone pulled at the wolf but to no avail. The cavern wall shattered and a towering black form stepped toward them. Mummified from millennia in the peat, every ripple of muscle and tendon and sinew stood out on its smooth surface. Danu's son swiveled its giant head in the direction of Moddey's howls. Its nostrils were nothing but holes in its head and its mouth a lipless maw.

Malone released Moddey Dhoo. "You'll be OK. It's not hunting you. We'll meet on the other side."

He willed his legs to run toward the cove. A squeal of pain and heartbreak followed his retreat. Malone turned back. The wolf's lit eyes reflected Malone's final moments of cowardice during the war. Running away. Running toward his illustrious future. The wolf managed a final cry of the betrayed before black fingers yanked him out of the hole.

"No!" Malone reversed course back into the cavern to see Danu's son, the mighty Caorthannach, clutching Moddey Dhoo around the throat. The wolf's limbs spasmed and his howls died out. He dangled from the bog man's clawed hand with lolling tongue.

The one true creature in this bloody place, and Danu let her son kill it. Malone's roar of outrage rose into a battle cry worthy of the Morrigan. He ran at the creature with the Sword of Light raised. He swung the sword, but the blade froze in midair.

This couldn't be. He'd almost died his submission was so complete. "What is the point of all of this?" he yelled.

His voice echoed back at him. He was truly on his own now. He grabbed the hilt with both hands and willed the Sword of Light to obey him, but it held fast. The bog man lurched toward him, sniffing, seeking.

Logic dictated that the sword must submit to him now. He swore he'd felt its acceptance like he'd felt his heart surge toward Nemain's hand. His thoughts fled in panic, not that it mattered. They were no use, anyhow. Old emotions flooded him instead, all that despair mixed with a stubborn will toward his own path and away from what his father and the village dictated for a poor Catholic lad. All those *emotions*. He'd submitted to them, understood his loneliness at the heart of it all.

No, it wasn't about submission, he realized, so much as acceptance. In their usual enigmatic, other crowd way, the questing beast and Cerridwen had masked the point. He'd made a choice. Long ago, on the day he'd rejected his sister's comfort, he'd really been rejecting himself. And that choice had shriveled his soul over the years into one that only allowed for ambition.

A thread of calm weaved its way through him and toward his fingertips touching the sword. He relaxed his grip and invited the sword to approach him. A surge of strength coursed through him. He swung the blade, fast as quicksilver, and sliced open the bog man's knee. The creature shrieked. Moddey landed near the cauldron in a furred heap.

Again, Malone swung the sword at the bog man's towering legs. Orange rays streaked through the wounds he opened in the leathery skin. He hacked at the limb in an effort to topple the creature like a giant tree. The bog man reached for him, and Malone dodged through its legs and ran toward Moddey.

"Moddey!" he yelled.

Dried-up fingers brushed Malone's back. He darted right and sank behind the Dagda's Cauldron. He waited for the bog man to spit fire as his name Caorthannach implied. Instead it bellowed a nonsensical jumble of consonants and vowels.

Malone peeked around the cauldron to witness Danu's son wailing and beating against the remaining sides of the cavern. Malone pressed his back against the golden cauldron. On a long exhale, he heaved and managed to shift the cauldron a few inches. His shoulder flared, forcing him to stop. As ever, his weakness defined him.

Around the curve of the cauldron he caught sight of Moddey. In death, he'd returned to his curly spaniel form, delicate and sweet, eyes open and dark, unwavering integrity snuffed out. A quiet fury filled Malone while above him the bog man crashed around destroying the rest of the cavern. He crouched again and this time used his weight to rock the cauldron. He relaxed and pushed again, and with each push, the rocking motion increased. He must hurry, but he couldn't hurry. He needed momentum, not brute force. He continued rocking the cauldron until its weight dragged it crashing to the floor.

The bog man's hideous wails of frustration died. Black eyeholes swiveled toward him.

The cauldron that forever replenished itself spilled its elixir, and within moments a golden stream that radiated a warm hue of health and bounty flowed around Moddey's body. Squinting against the dazzle, Malone rushed toward the dog. He splashed knee deep into the rising stream and cupped his hand beneath Moddey's muzzle.

"Drink," he said. "Curse you, drink."

Malone froze as the bog man lurched in his direction and stopped to sniff the air. Malone squatted in front of the creature, yet it couldn't pick him out from within the Dagda's stream. The liquid's radiance must camouflage him. He held Moddey's head with mouth open and forced liquid into the dog's mouth.

"Come on, come on," he muttered as the bog man leaned out, sniffing, seeking, over the cauldron's stream, which was more like a river now. Malone dunked under the surface until the bog man's focus shifted away from him again. It hunted along the edge of the river yet avoided wetting its feet in the cauldron's magic.

Malone filled Moddey's mouth, clamped his jaw shut, and raised his head. Let gravity work to drip the liquid down the dog's esophagus. He shook Moddey's head in futility and frustration. "What's the good of the Dagda's Cauldron?" he hissed.

He released Moddey's head, and it sank, first the nose, then muzzle, eyes, one ear. He caught a movement from the second ear as it submerged. Frantic, he dove under the surface, grabbed hold of Moddey's body, and dragged it to a shallower area. His shoulder jabbed at him as he held the dog's head again. Moddey's ear twitched.

"You can do it," Malone whispered.

Through his hands, he felt Moddey's throat muscles constrict and relax. Swallowing. His eyelids trembled, and then his body shuddered on a great heave and he sprang to his feet in the shallows, alert and with floppy ears perked.

So that was the way the Dagda's Cauldron was supposed to work. Moddey was worthy of its power, that much was obvious.

The bog man swung toward them. Malone pulled on Moddey's leg, "Come here. Back into the river."

They paddled to the center where the current was strongest. The bog man's gaze passed over them again.

Holding on to Moddey, Malone let the flow carry them where it would.

Chapter Twenty-Two

The river flowed down a slope toward the back of the cavern where the bog man had crashed its way in. The current hurled them through a series of stone corridors that ended with a cascade out of a square window. Malone landed on the ground and the river receded back to a stream, then a trickle, then droplets. Cerridwen or one of the others must have returned and righted the cauldron. Maybe they kept an immortal's scorecard of his progress. Of course they did.

Malone blinked up at the Milky Way and Big Dipper. He could melt into the earth his relief was so great. Here was ground he knew, just as he recognized the stone walls that surrounded him. Peel Castle. He also knew this particular raw damp from winds off the Irish Sea. Goosebumps rose on his naked chest and arms as he inhaled the scent of brine and moss and bonfires. After the strangely temperature-less other world, the top world's chill seeped into his bones.

"Moddey?" he called.

His guide had vanished along with the Dagda's elixir and the Sword of Light. Malone wasn't sure whether to feel reassured or disappointed. He decided on reassured. Perhaps saving Moddey's life had earned him a reprieve. One act of selflessness within a barren life.

However, now he would never experience the Spear of Lugh, the warrior hero elevated to god-hood, whose spear was said to always hit its target. He would not feel it in his grip, wield its surefire focus. However, he would sleep in his own bed until he awoke, whether that be hours or days or weeks from now.

Clutching his shoulder, he force-marched himself across the main castle compound and toward the entrance. The gates stood open. Malone trudged along the causeway that led from the tiny island Peel Castle sat on to the mainland. Bonfires covered the hillsides. So, little or no time had passed in this world. He was too depleted to be surprised.

He grabbed a tattered horse blanket off the back of a wagon and draped it over his shoulders. The smell of horse reminded him of the pooka. He shuddered and shook his head to rid himself of that visual. Better to imagine the fair selkie.

Rather than head to his cottage, he continued through the village toward the old cart trail that led to the excavation site. Blessed silence kept him company except for the murmuring tide and gusting wind. The hawthorn he'd almost chopped down stood out against the night sky, a scraggly excuse for a tree. Malone resigned himself to leaving the hawthorn where it stood. He'd find another way—a more costly and time-consuming way, no doubt— to extract the bog body from the ground, if it was there at all. He must know either way.

Lost in thought, he ignored his exhaustion until he arrived at the trench and sank to his knees. The scent of horse and fresh-dug earth, the soggy ground saturating his jeans, the susurration of the tide against the shore. Yes, this was home.

He opened his eyes and stared into the night, past the nearest bonfires and toward the moonlit water. The wind died. The Samhain bonfires glowed without revelers attending them. In fact, he detected no human presence at all. No last quiet conversations around the bonfires. No late-night music from the houses below him. No lights either.

He studied the night sky again. Prickles rose on the back of his neck and his heartbeat accelerated. The stars were nothing but pricked holes in a vast black blanket. Another sky that was not a sky. Danu had sucker-punched him with this elaborate set created just for him. She wasn't done with him yet.

Malone peered into the trench. Empty except for tangled hawthorn roots that followed the outline of the bog man's body, cushioning the creature through eternity.

Jumbled thoughts scratched out the insides of Malone's head like mice making juice of his brains. Then thought fled altogether as a mounting terror crept up his spine.

A slither and crackle.

"Moddey?" he said.

A low rumble seeped in beneath the sound of the ocean. The hawthorn's bark shifted and churned, and its branches twisted around themselves. Malone craned his neck as the hawthorn rose to tower three stories over his head. From the trench, the roots extended toward Malone and wrapped themselves around his legs.

From high in the tree a sinuous voice floated over him. "The good ghost dog of Peel Castle has discharged its duty to bring you full circle."

Anticipation and dread mounted a steady internal scream inside Malone's body. The inevitable approach of Caorthannach paled in comparison to the threat that Abhartach posed to him. He couldn't take his eyes off the hawthorn tree with its skeletal branches. His teeth chattered as he imagined the blood drinker dangling up there like a bat.

Maybe the point had always been about Abhartach, not Danu's bog child.

"Here I am," Abhartach said.

Malone jerked. Too close, the ghoul lurked too bloody close. His sweet breath coated Malone's senses. More roots wrapped themselves around his waist, sinuous and tickling, only they weren't roots, were they?

Abhartach stepped around Malone without releasing his embrace. Malone's body shook in mortal fear of this creature. More so than with the bog man or Danu or the pooka or the questing beast. And all the more so because the hanging man was no longer hanging. In fact, rope no longer bound his feet at all. He stood free while Malone's feet were bound. In this reversal, Abhartach's power over Malone was complete.

Abhartach's teeth glowed in the moonlight when he smiled. Malone tilted away from the teeth and the smile and the warmth, but the arms held him seemingly everywhere around his body at once.

Malone found his voice at last. "You're free."

"I was never captive." Abhartach rubbed his cheek against Malone's and whispered into his ear. "Things aren't what they seem here as I'm sure you've noticed."

Abhartach tightened his grip so that Malone couldn't look away if he'd tried. He leaned in and kissed Malone. A lingering kiss that tasted of the blood that coated his lips. Malone writhed away from the taste of spatter and the image of flying body parts.

"You loved Lonan Ward and you betrayed him," Abhartach said.

Malone squirmed but Abhartach held him fast. "No …"

"No?" Abhartach cocked his head with a bemused smile. "The love? Or the betrayal? Which do you deny? Because you can only deny one."

"I'm not—"

"Oh, but your preference for the female form didn't stop you from seducing Lonan, did it? You read his inclination so well." Abhartach thrust himself against Malone hard enough for Malone to feel him against his thigh. Despite himself, arousal flushed his skin. That nick of a moment he'd put out of his mind—in the barn, the two of them the only survivors in a burned-out village, that moment of isolation and terror, obsession and taboo.

"Besides," Abhartach whispered, "love is love, it matters not the body it comes with."

Abhartach's warmth soaked into Malone's being. He bowed his head and leaned his full weight on the man-thing before him. Abhartach propped him up while Malone's mind drifted away. He barely felt Abhartach's bite.

Malone spoke the truth. "It wasn't love."

Abhartach pulled away and held Malone's head between his hands. Blood dripped off his teeth and down his chin. His lips glistened. "So you admit to betraying Lonan."

"No love, but tenderness. Lonan found solace in that before he died."

Abhartach's expression hardened. "Which makes your betrayal and his death a hundred times worse. Better you had tortured the location of the bog man out of him than pretend at pretty emotions you didn't feel."

He stepped back and vanished along with the roots that bound Malone's feet to the ground. Abhartach's voice floated around him. "Choose your mark well."

Malone retched against the taste of blood and defilement and self-loathing. He pictured Lonan, the way his eyes had lit up when Malone kissed him for the first time. The puppy who'd looked up to Malone's seniority, who'd reacted like a lovesick fool and revealed the final piece of information that Malone sought: the exact location of the bog man. Lonan had entrusted Malone with the island's secret as he would a lover. And then later Malone had convinced himself that it was too late to save Lonan when he ran away from the burning barn. In truth, Malone could have shifted the beam that pinned Lonan and supported him as they fled the enemy troops that had infiltrated the village. Could have, but all he saw was his future, a future made more beautiful than any flowering May tree by his success. He coveted the bog man for himself.

No one would know that Malone had chosen the bog man over Lonan. No one would know that in a split second he'd decided that Lonan was expendable in the face of achieving his future free and clear. He'd turned away from Lonan's beseeching and then betrayed gaze. The light drained out of his eyes well before the enemy executed him. The *rat-a-tat* of their guns and Lonan's screams pursued Malone as he fled.

He'd killed Lonan as surely as if he'd shot him himself.

At long last, Malone understood. Danu and the other crowd had it in for him because of Lonan's death, not digging up the bog man. The way Lonan had died, how Malone had used him and cast him away to save his own life. Malone's life a straight and steady line of opportunism that culminated in Lonan's death.

He wiped his lips with the back of his hand. The question was what made Lonan so special.

Malone straightened to see an image floating beyond his reach. A gift from Abhartach. One image this time. He managed to grab hold of it for a few seconds before it scattered into the night.

The Queen of Wands with her piercing gaze and sharpened staff. Danu.

Chapter Twenty-Three

Shaking from his encounter with Abhartach, Malone surveyed the view toward Peel Castle and the jagged Manxian coastline. Fog curled in with the waves and softened sharp edges in an attempt to fool Malone into believing that monsters didn't dwell within the shadows. But he knew better.

He concentrated on what lurked below the song of the tides and the telltale thud of Caorthannach's approach, but he heard nothing. The bonfires on the neighboring hillsides burned in silence. No hiss, no crackle. They had grown large enough to throw their shadows onto Malone and the hawthorn. The flames licked up into a sky that wasn't a sky and shed a macabre glow over this facsimile of the top world.

Fear pricked at him; he'd always distrusted the quiet on the battlefield. The lull in combat caused his mind to attack itself like crazed ants overwhelming prey. Malone pressed a hand against his chest and tried to calm his erratic heartbeat. He'd been here before, to this consigned place of turmoil and terror, with no choice in the matter but to obey orders and fling himself into the nightmare.

He must find the fourth wand. He'd passed the tests for the Sword of Light, the Stone of Destiny, and the Dagda's Cauldron. Now for the Spear of Lugh.

Abhartach had warned him to choose his mark well, which must mean the spear that never missed its mark hid nearby. He cast about in search of a hiding spot and caught sight of the Sword of Light under the hawthorn tree. A surge of relief lightened his limbs.

The horse blanket lay where it had fallen off his shoulders when Abhartach arrived. He rolled up the blanket into a skinny tube, then sliced open a few layers of the fabric and slid the sword into its makeshift sheath. He slung the sheath over his back and tied the ends around his torso.

Now, to find the Spear of Lugh. He knelt at the head of the trench where hawthorn roots tangled within the peat. Perhaps the hawthorn protected the spear as it had protected the bog man. Malone tugged boggy material from between the roots, careful not to damage the tree itself. Sweat dripped down his face and his eyes stung with bonfire smoke.

A low rumble from the bowels of the earth shook the ground beneath Malone. The peat roiled beneath his feet. He scrambled out of the trench and backed into the hawthorn. Around him, the bonfires expanded and entrapped him in a ring of fire. A classic move in warfare. He clenched his fists against the tremors. No. He refused to allow the old combat stress to affect him.

Grasping hawthorn branches spread vast above him. He ignored the jabs his shoulder threw out as he hoisted himself onto the lowest limb. High into the hawthorn Malone climbed until he found a spot to hunker where two branches formed a juncture. The bonfires spat flames. Heat flushed his skin.

The fabric of time ripped apart, and a crevasse opened with a roar of flames that shot thirty feet into the air. Malone ducked his head against their heat and watched through tearing eyes as a black form coalesced out of flames. Danu. Her tunic flowed around her and the sun shield on her chest reflected flame light like a great eye. Her beast of a son crawled out after her. A stupid creature, Malone now saw, with no will of its own.

Danu tilted her head to look up at Malone. He braced himself for her next move in this vast game she had orchestrated. For what purpose, he still didn't comprehend.

The circle of flames bent toward Danu as if feeding off her energy. More flames licked up her body and she grew bright within them. The staff that she held glowed. With a graceful movement she raised the staff and faced her son. Malone stared, uncomprehending, as Danu lifted her arm and with one fluid thrust buried the staff deep into the bog man's chest. The bog man screamed and burst into blue flames. When they died back, Danu grew in their place, a goddess of the fire. If anything, her beauty increased, her penetrating eyes as large and brown as the selkie's but filled with ferocity.

"You killed your own son," Malone said.

She acknowledged his words with a small and perfect smile. Her voice pure like dew drops floated toward him. "Never. I would protect him at all costs. You survived him against the odds, and now it's time for him to sleep again."

"Why didn't you send him back to sleep in the first place then?"

"Because you didn't deserve my favor."

Danu tossed her staff into the air. Malone tensed, but she caught it and thumped the ground. This was the thud Malone had heard all along. Danu, not the bog man. Danu, marching her son toward Malone.

"You can't stay up there forever. You must finish what you started." Danu held out her arms with the staff balanced across her palms. "Come and get it."

The staff's twin-pointed ends glinted sharp as glass shards, their razor-sharp tips silver-edged in the heat of the fire within which Danu still stood. The Spear of Lugh.

With growing horror, Malone observed the way her dark eyes continued reflecting the flames when she stepped out of them, and the way her skin glowed like molten glaze. She thumped the spear on the ground and the earth rolled closed. Malone wrapped his legs around the trunk and held on.

"Do you comprehend?" she said.

She raised the hand not carrying the spear and blew on her fingers until they started to glow and a ball of fire sat in her palm. Whip fast, she launched the red-hot ball toward him. Malone ducked and felt the impact of the ball against the tree trunk where his head had rested moments before. The tree keened with thousands of rustling leaves.

"Fire spitter," Malone said. "Caorthannach."

"One of my many names. The Devil's mother, as you top worlders say in your usual imprecise fashion. Or Mother of the Gods. Or Danu. It matters not."

She shot another fire ball at him, and the hawthorn recoiled upon impact.

"You would destroy the sacred tree?" he said.

"I'm surprised you care. You would have destroyed it with no more thought than you destroyed Lonan Ward."

The tree rocked back as another incoming fireball burned a hole in its bark. Malone shuddered in reaction to the orange glow, the smoke, the hawthorn's agonized wailing. He shifted around the trunk away from Danu's projectiles and pressed the side of his head against the warm bark. He tried to close his ears to keening from deep within the tree. Or his memories. He wasn't sure. His own boyish weeping echoed through the bark, and a sigh whispered out of a knot hole, a whiff of a voice. Lonan. "You ended us."

"I don't understand."

"You were supposed to save me."

"I'm sorry." Malone peered around the trunk to see her hefting the Spear of Lugh. "Stop!" he yelled.

Danu drew her arm back in a graceful arc and let the spear fly. The spear lifted into the air, a fire lit streak that arced toward the hawthorn. Malone swung around the trunk and drew the Sword of Light from its makeshift sheath. He held the blade out toward the oncoming spear. Its luminosity caught and shone like a lamp, and the spear wobbled. Malone imagined the spear with its intense focus aiming toward itself as reflected off the sword's broad blade. The hawthorn quaked. Malone sensed its fear and crawled out on a limb toward the oncoming spear. His body quivered with effort to hold the sword in place, to face Danu's final onslaught without cowering.

The Spear of Lugh crashed into the sword, piercing its own reflection. A booming shockwave almost toppled Malone out of the tree. A moment later, the Sword of Light melted from Malone's hand to be replaced by the Spear of Lugh.

Chapter Twenty-Four

Malone clutched the Spear of Lugh to his body, savoring the sleek feel of it in his hands. Perfectly weighted, light yet dense. The optimal throwing weapon. The fourth wand.

"Very good," Danu said. "You may do, after all."

"For what?" Malone said. "Tell me what this is about!"

Malone tucked the spear into the makeshift sheath and reversed his way back along the limb toward the trunk. Burn holes scarred the hawthorn, and when Malone pressed his ear against the bark, a boy's sobbing continued to echo out of the past. He'd consigned himself to a similar prison long ago, true, but his boyhood self didn't belong to this place. No part of him did.

"Don't be so sure about that," Danu said.

The roar from the circle of flames filled his head as he climbed down the branches and dropped to the ground. Danu appeared as he'd first met her with penetrating gaze and hair flowing over the breastplate of her tunic. He stepped toward her while pulling the spear out of the sheath again. Danu smiled. The flames around them grew taller and shadowed cores within them moved of their own accords.

"I survived the challenge of the Four Wands," he said. "The treasures of the Tuatha Dé Danann yielded to me." He leveled the spear at Danu. "The Sword of Light that submitted to me, the Stone of Destiny that accepted me, the Dagda's Cauldron that revived me, and now I'll win any engagement with the Spear of Lugh."

"If you know what you're fighting for," Danu said. "If the goal is true."

He sprinted the short distance to the trench and leapt toward the bog man, who lay as an inert artifact once again. He ignored the ache in his shoulder and raised the spear with both hands so that the tip pointed at the bog man's chest. He'd outwitted this world, had demonstrated his resilience. He'd won. In all ways, he'd won, yet here he remained, trapped.

"I will kill your son, make no mistake. Let me go. I won your little game."

Danu's expression hardened. The fire within her eyes brightened again, reminding Malone of Moddey Dhoo. In one whip-like movement she snapped a fire ball in his direction. Malone dropped to the ground next to the bog man.

Danu approached and stood at the head of the trench. Her eyes smoldered with malevolence. Malone shifted the spear so that once again its tip touched the bog man.

"It seems we are at an impasse," he said.

"I'm not," she said, "but you are. There's a little known rule about the spear. Little known to your kind, anyhow. *Duine* who claim the spear, must use the spear in a true purpose. Once aimed for battle, you must throw it. Don't let go of it until then."

"Or else what?"

Danu pointed to the sharpened end of the spear that pointed away from her son, that, in fact, pointed toward Malone himself. "It will turn on you."

Of course. Nothing was straightforward in the other world. He repositioned the spear between his body and the bog man's body so that it pointed at neither of them. "I haven't finished the wand tests then," he said. "The Spear of Lugh is still before me."

"Indeed. You have come far though. A great feat in itself, but you face a difficult decision." Danu didn't raise her voice. She never did, but it rang out like a bell. "I know my true cause." She swept her arm to encompass the other world. "Continuity. Do you have a true cause unrelated to your self-interests?"

Malone ignored the question in favor of considering the word "continuity." Continuity of her line, obviously—the bog man—whom she wanted to remain tucked in peat for eternity, not laid out under scientists' lamps and poked and prodded, not used by the likes of Malone to make a name for himself. Malone understood this now but, nevertheless, assumed they could arrive at a compromise. Reveal the find to the world while at the same time marking it as a sacred preservation site not to be disturbed.

Danu's laughter rose above the roar of the flames. Her ridicule filled his head, like his father's laughter, meant to scourge. He crawled out of the trench and stood before Danu with spear pressing against her chest. The spear hissed on contact.

Danu raised her head toward the sky that was not a sky and tilted her head back in a parody of ecstasy. She leaned into the spear. "As you will. If you dare."

Within the wall of flame, black forms forged by Danu's fire took shape. Malone gripped the spear tighter against the stink from a thousand furnaces. Smoke curled around them, causing Malone's eyes to water. Through his tears, the black forms solidified, and one by one they stepped out of the flames. Dozens of Danus burnished by flame encircled him, taunting him to choose his target well.

The real Danu's eyes shone brighter than the fires. She raised her hand and blew on her fingers. Malone stood close enough to see a snake-like hiss of flame gather in her palm. Her hand whipped out and behind Malone, the hawthorn cried out with creaking limbs. She paused, and then hurled another fire ball. Branches overhead convulsed and curled in on themselves in their suffering.

Danu's replicas circled closer to Malone. If he killed the original, the rest of them would surely melt away, but Danu of the flesh flew out of reach beyond the circle and continued attacking the hawthorn. A plaintive boyish voice cried without solace. Malone felt the tug of him. He'd save that brave boy who'd found joy in small moments while digging in dirt.

Danu's creatures surrounded him. He raised the spear. Their faces melted into new facades. Abhartach's sly smile and blood dripping mouth. "You!" Malone said, and lunged, but then the face slid away again to be replaced by Danu's. Malone turned in circles. The replicas' faces slipped past him pliable as putty, reforming themselves like a carousel of the damned. Cerridwen. Ilios. Lonan with beseeching gaze.

"No," Malone said. "Not you. You're not here."

He continued circling. They weren't alive, he reminded himself. Figments, all of them. Anghus, grieving. Nemain. Even the questing beast's snake head morphed out of one of the visages before melting away again. A pixie face with dimples. Maggie. She'd never comforted him again after that day under the May tree. His rejection was that complete and unshakeable.

The spear twitched in Malone's grip, its internal forces craved action, but it knew no focus without Malone's true intent to back it up. Abhartach had warned him. Malone must choose his mark well.

Lonan swirled past, imploring him again. "You ended us," he said before his face slid away, replaced by the pooka's horse nostrils and white-ringed eyes.

The smoke grew thicker. Malone ran from one replica to the next. Abhartach flickered past. "Your turn next."

Malone caught himself before driving the spear toward that hateful face. So close, but he wasn't sure. The spear jerked in his grip, and he grabbed hold of it with both hands lest it tear itself away from him with or without his consent. He hissed with mounting fury as he continued to circle along with the kaleidoscope of faces. He must understand his truth. That was all. The spear would find its focus based on his truth.

"Abhartach!" Malone roared. "My turn for what?"

The blood drinker slid into focus and stepped out of the circle, all sinuous grace and mocking smile. He flitted forward and grabbed Malone from behind in a grip both vicelike and tender. The press of him against Malone's back seared into him, igniting him with a kind of clarity as his body began to shake.

"My turn for what?" Malone repeated.

Abhartach bent Malone's head back. His lips pressed into Malone's neck near the previous puncture wounds. He lingered there for a long moment. "To be the continuity," he whispered.

Abhartach rocked with Malone in a tortured dance that swung them toward the hawthorn tree, now with bark scorched from Danu's fire and branches sagging toward the ground. Abhartach hugged him closer until Malone couldn't think over arousal and revulsion at war once again—the way he'd betrayed Lonan in every stroke of Abhartach's fingers. Taunting him with his betrayal.

Abhartach rested his chin on Malone's shoulder. His voice caressed Malone's ear. "The tree dies without continuity."

The smoke parted and Malone spied a small shadow hunched against the side of the tree. A sobbing boy. Cerridwen had mentioned a glimmer worth saving within Malone, and there it was. Abhartach's arms melted away from him, the hissing voices within the flames died back. In the quiet space between thoughts, Malone raised the Spear of Lugh and let it fly.

CHAPTER TWENTY-FIVE

Malone shot up with heart hammering and a scream caught in his throat. He patted himself down in a desperate attempt to verify his existence, his mind elsewhere amidst shrieking artillery shells and screams and glowing eyes and—

"No," he told the figments, and scrambled out of bed. His legs gave out on him, and he landed on his knees.

Combat stress, he reminded himself. He was familiar with the sensation of careening out of sleep like the hounds of hell were upon him.

Hounds of hell. Moddey Dhoo.

"Holy Christ," he groaned.

He climbed onto the bed to catch his breath. He wore baggy pajama bottoms and nothing else. He rubbed his hands over the familiar flannel and studied his torso, the concave stomach and pattern of ribs up to his jutting collarbones. Wasted away no different than during the war. He raised one arm. A jolt of pain coursed through his shoulder. He dropped his arm again.

One more self-check—the injury he hoped not to find, because if it didn't exist he might be sane and there might be a rational explanation. He closed his eyes against the image of Abhartach and ran his fingers over his neck. Smooth skin except for two scabbed puncture wounds where the blood drinker had tasted him.

Malone rocked back and forth with eyes closed, humming tunelessly. He knew what he'd survived in the other world, but he wasn't sure what had actually *happened*. If that made sense. He wasn't sure it did. He longed to burrow himself into the darkest, safest corner of his mind.

He forced his eyes open to survey his surroundings. First order of business, orient himself. Unfortunately, he didn't recognize the room. Simple and spare with white walls and a few pieces of well-made but old oak furniture. Above the dresser a black blanket hung over what Malone guessed to be a mirror. A mourning house.

Rosy strands of late afternoon sunlight lit up a jaunty hook rug. Well-washed and lively. Malone inventoried the other signs of hominess. The soft quilt he sat upon. The lace curtains wafting in a breeze from the cracked window.

A home, yes.

Through the window he caught sight of a jagged shoreline, dryrock walls, and there, off to the side, one of Peel Castle's fortified walls. The Isle of Man. Although this might not be the Isle of Man. This might be another ruse, a far more realistic ruse with fresh rain and a sky that looked like a sky.

Thud.

Malone jerked upright. The muscles in his throat caught. He couldn't have screamed if he'd tried.

Thud.

He crawled across the bed toward the dresser. Ignoring the jab from his shoulder, he yanked out one of the drawers and tossed aside folded clothes. His clothes.

Thud.

He held the drawer over his head in a defensive posture. His muscles jittered with the effort. He stumbled and caught himself as the thuds stopped in front of his door. The door creaked open.

Malone swung at the shadow that crossed the threshold.

Anghus pulled the drawer from Malone's sagging grip. "Whoa now, laddie. Watch where you're swinging that thing."

"That you, Anghus?"

"Who else would I be?" Anghus helped Malone back to the bed. "Now that you're awake, you'll be needing food. A big evening ahead."

Malone grabbed Anghus's spindly arm. "Do you know what happened to me?"

Anghus's crinkles reminded Malone of Cerridwen, and his gaze held similar wisdom. "I do, but you're fine. Give it time, and you'll see."

"How did I get here?"

"The other crowd returned you as I hoped they would. I weren't sure of it, you know. Waiting and hoping."

"But—"

"We cleaned you up, gave you a drought, and you've been sleeping like the dead until now." He shook his head in pity. "I'd have not been you for the life of me. Themselves are not to be trusted until the exact moment you can trust them. Enough for now. Come along for a meal when you're dressed."

Anghus's footsteps retreated toward the front of the cottage. He'd left the bedroom door open, for which Malone was grateful. With a start, he realized that this must be Lonan's bedroom.

Malone stood on wobbly feet and made his way to a pile of clothes on the floor. Slow as a recovering war victim, he fished out jeans and a jumper, and pulled them on. His stomach grumbled in response to the scents of coffee and sizzling meat that filtered into the room. He found socks and shoes, and after putting them on, passed more covered mirrors on his way to the kitchen.

Anghus laid a plate filled with fried eggs, grilled tomatoes and blood sausages before Malone. "Take it slow. Themselves barely kept you alive."

Anghus's matter-of-fact acceptance of the other world steadied Malone, as if they were talking about a football game that had turned a bit rowdy.

Malone raised a forkful of eggs to his mouth, but his stomach heaved. He lowered the fork.

"You must eat," Anghus said.

Malone forced down the eggs and started to feel less hollowed out. "You said 'we.' Who brought me back?"

"Dunno any name he goes by, but he visits now and then as needed. Man in a long, black robe with a giant hood. A druid, I expect. Carrying you into my house like a baby, with you draped like the dead. Gave me a start, it did, until I saw you were alive. He helped me settle you, and then—*poof*—gone." He shrugged. "The way of him. A magician, like."

"Not Danu then."

Anghus's face lit with a broad smile. He chortled. "Bloody hell, no! The likes of her up top, never. She pulls her strings from the other world. Need to beware of her."

"So I learned." Malone's stomach churned again. He pushed away his plate with food half eaten. Details emerged from the endless orange glow of fire. The Four Wands and the four challenges. He'd managed to survive them all, but the outcome still felt unfinished.

"Ay now." Anghus patted Malone's hand before clearing away his plate. "You'll remember soon enough.

Your aim was true with the Spear of Lugh, that's all you'll be needing to know for now."

"So I'm finished, just like that."

Anghus *hmmm*'d and placed a cup of coffee in front of Malone. Malone savored the smell, so long gone, so recently back into their lives since rations ended.

"Anghus, I—" He stopped, unable to put words around his regrets, his remorse. For the first time, he noticed Anghus's resemblance to Lonan in the distance between his eyes and slope of his nose. "I'll put a stop to the dig. The bog man should remain undisturbed."

"I'm glad to hear you say it, although I'll never forgive you for leaving Lonan to die."

"How do you know about that?"

"All will become clear soon enough." He studied Malone. His expression brightened as if Malone were a feast for his eyes. "You'll find some things have sorted themselves. You're in no danger unless you do something stupid."

Chapter Twenty-Six

Several hours later, after Malone threw up his meal and fell asleep again, he let Anghus bundle him into a thick wool coat and lead him outside into the long twilight. He drank in the purple-tinged vista over the Irish Sea as Anghus handed him a stout walking stick. Sunny yellow buttercups and cowslips bobbed along the edge of the lane.

Frowning, Malone pivoted back toward the house. He pointed to the hawthorn branches hanging beside the front door. Their frothy pink flowers and singular decaying scent almost made him gag. "Are you trying to drive me mad?"

Anghus held him by the shoulders and angled him away from the door. He spoke with careful neutrality. "It's May Day. Today we celebrate Beltane. Another day close to the veil. If themselves hadn't returned you today, they never would have."

Malone bowed his head and swallowed against lingering nausea. Six months gone.

Anghus guided him toward the lane with grip on his elbow. "Time runs differently in the other world."

"I'm tired. I'd rather not celebrate May Day."

"But you must."

Anghus's cottage stood fifty yards off the village square. Doors stood open to the evening and light streamed out of the cottages and shops. Hawthorn branches and wreaths made of marsh marigolds adorned the buildings. In front of the church, a maypole stood with festive ribbons shifting in the breeze. Malone stood for a moment, remembering the long ago day he'd banished tears.

"Come," Anghus said.

Further on, a caeli band had set up shop. Music and laughter skipped around on the breeze while villagers swung around each other and children dashed in and out of the dancers. Two young women waved toward Anghus and Malone and started toward them. Anghus waylaid them, and with a few words and nods from the women, he sent them on their way.

Leaning on the cane, Malone noticed the way the villagers smiled and beckoned, inviting him into their midst. A few men clapped him on the back as they passed like he was an old friend. The two women peeked back at him, their avid expressions making him uneasy. They must know he was risen from the other crowd. Maybe the whole village was in on the secret of the bog man.

"Come," Anghus said. "You can join the festivities later, if you like."

"Where are we going?"

Anghus pointed toward hillsides dotted with bonfires once again. Malone pulled way.

"I'm afraid you must," Anghus said.

Humans, not the other crowd, manned these flames, Malone reminded himself. No harm would come from these fires, no shadowy beings ready to step out of them at Danu's bidding. Still, he gripped the cane hard as he stepped forward with Anghus.

Twenty grueling minutes later, Malone leaned against Anghus's slight but sinewy form as they approached the hawthorn that protected the bog man. Someone had built a bonfire here, too. The flames cast a festive glow over hundreds of pink blossoms. Meadow rue and grass tussocks grew undisturbed over the bog man's burial spot.

"For years, the faery tree languished," Anghus said, "but now it thrives again. A sign that all will be well."

Malone perched where Anghus indicated on one of two stumps sitting near the bonfire. Anghus sat next to him. Malone tucked his feet against the stump, not trusting the flames.

"Does everyone know what happened?" Malone said.

Firelight cast an orange glow over Anghus's features. Malone averted his gaze toward the ground.

"In a way, yes. We have our customs. There's an understanding between us and the locals."

Us. Malone's apprehension increased. For several minutes silence reigned between the two men. Finally, Anghus said, "I have brilliant news and not-so-brilliant news."

Malone blinked into the blue core within the bonfire.

"The brilliant news," Anghus continued, "is that you proved yourself worthy."

"Worthy," Malone spat. "Do tell."

"That's the not-so-brilliant news. Or rather, you might consider it bad news. In reality, it's more good news."

Malone gripped the walking stick harder still. "Cough it up, old man."

Anghus glanced at him. "It might be better if—"

He nodded toward the bonfire. The flames rose and its blue core darkened and grew into a human-like form. Malone stumbled to his feet with every nerve ending in his body propelling him to flee. He swung the walking stick at Anghus and spun away to leave this infernal island with its superstitions and rituals. A hand landed on his shoulder and yanked him around so quickly he stumbled again.

Abhartach's bloodied chin was visible within a deep hood attached to a flowing black robe. Terror betrayed Malone's instincts. He stood paralyzed as he peered into the darkness within the cowl. Abhartach's glistening mouth smiled with invitation.

"Leave me the fecking hell alone," Malone said. "I'm done with the lot of you."

Abhartach bowed his head. A moment later he pulled back the hood to reveal a man with sharp blue eyes and strong jawline.

"We needed to know you," the man said, "from your worst self."

Now Malone understood, all right. This man posing as Abhartach had reflected Malone back to himself—seducing Malone into submission just as he had seduced Lonan.

The magician, or druid, or whatever he was within the other world led Malone back to his seat beside the bonfire. Anghus stood aside while the magician sat beside Malone.

"We've been awaiting your arrival for years. We can be as patient as nature itself."

"Quit with the riddles. We're not in the other world anymore."

"As you wish." The magician didn't mince words. "You were doomed for a reckoning with the other crowd the moment you killed Lonan."

Malone scrubbed at his face, weary almost beyond his ability to cope. Lonan. "Not because I hacked at the hawthorn or woke the bog man."

"That didn't help," Anghus said. "Themselves took it out on you a little more for those actions. It's a miracle you survived."

Malone snorted. "Danu would have sicced her son on me no matter what."

"Not true," the magician said. "You brought that on yourself, as you did everything else."

"You haven't told me the bad news."

The magician placed a hand on Malone's forehead, and with a jolt, images flashed through his head. The Spear of Lugh raised within the shifting faces of the Danu replicas. Abhartach standing on his own, observing. The hawthorn and the sobbing child. The spear flying toward the child and piercing it in a blinding flash, and then Danu and Abhartach nodding in agreement. "He will do," Abhartach had said.

It seemed this being, the magician who had overseen Malone's journey through the other world had the final say on him.

"I killed myself," Malone said.

"No, you freed yourself for a more worthy life. That boy resides within you again."

As he surveyed the untrammeled ground before him, Malone realized that the driving need to succeed had withered, but now he felt adrift. Unmoored without the core of himself he'd held on to for so long.

"You are more for this life now," the magician said, "rather than living in fantasies of the future. Your life was a grand delusion. Now, it's not. There's peace in that."

"Is that right? Kind of you to say."

Malone stood, ready to depart the Isle of Man and good bloody riddance. He'd find his life again. He could still travel and join the exploration for knowledge. Perhaps Chile next. The black mummies of the Chinchorro people fascinated him. He needed a purpose in life. The accursed other crowd hadn't burned that out of him.

Anghus sighed. The magician appraised Malone with a neutral expression before stepping back into the fire. "No, you are one of us now."

"The hell I am."

Malone walked away. Anghus followed. They trod down the hill and through the village. The dancing mayhem was in full swing. Malone ignored the greetings that drifted toward him. He'd get a decent night's sleep and plan his next steps tomorrow.

Anghus caught up with him outside his cottage.

"Has no one wondered where I've been these past six months?" Malone said.

"Did you leave anyone behind who would?" Anghus smiled, but with a worried expression. "You'll find your way, and if it's work you'll be craving, there's other local history to be found on the island." He grabbed Malone's arm. "You can't leave. Best to face this fact."

Malone yanked back his arm. "Danu isn't around to stop me." He placed his hand on the door knob and paused at the sound of scratching. "What is that?"

"Listen here." Anghus stepped in front of Malone to block the doorway. "You've not heard it all yet."

More scratching rattled the door followed by an excited *yip*. Malone pushed Anghus aside. "Move the bloody hell out of my way."

"There's the Ward bloodline, you see," Anghus said. "In one form or another, we've lived here for millennia to protect the sacred spot on the hillside. You killed the end of the line, my son Lonan. You ended us."

From within the house, a howl rose into the night. The hairs on the back of Malone's neck stood on end. He shoved at Anghus, but the old man held his ground with back braced against the door.

"Listen to me—" Anghus started, but Moddey Dhoo's howls rose again. Plaintive and yearning. Malone felt their lament in his chest. Revelry from the village square quieted, everyone listening, Malone imagined, with heads cocked, understanding the truth that still eluded him.

"What trick is this?" Malone said.

"No trick."

Anghus opened the door and a coal black spaniel with a curly coat and floppy ears leapt out with an excited bark. Laughter and music rose from the square once again. Moddey wriggled and jumped against Malone with a great doggy smile on his face. Malone stroked the dog's silky head and received licks in return. "Nice to see you again, boy," Malone murmured.

Anghus stepped backwards into the house while he spoke. "There's something to be said for living a simple life. Marrying, having children. Family and friends. A community tied to the land and its history. There's no call to feel lonely in a life like this."

Malone buried his hands in Moddey's fur to hide their shaking. A thready pulse beat in his neck.

Anghus pulled a black cloth off a mirror hanging beside the door. "In time you will appreciate the honor bestowed on you. Themselves could have killed you instead."

He unhooked the mirror from the wall. Malone clenched his hands, pulling Moddey's fur in the process. The dog whined and licked Malone's hand.

"Moddey's been lonely these last years since you killed Lonan. He's companion to the last in the line until the birth of the next heir, and then becomes the companion to that person. Moddey Dhoo only shows himself for us Wards, you see."

Anghus swiveled the mirror toward Malone. Lonan's freckled reflection blinked back at him, expression uncomprehending at first before it widened into the same horror Malone remembered before he turned his back on Lonan for the final time.

"No," he said.

"Yes," Anghus said. "Themselves found you worthy."

Malone had survived the other world, been found fit for this—a life of penance. To gaze upon his treachery every day for the rest of his life. To be a prisoner inside another man's existence.

"Themselves won't let you leave," Anghus said, "because you might never return. There's value to come of it, though, as the next in the Ward bloodline. The new heir."

Below the hum of music and tides, Malone caught other sounds. The slither of blackened limbs shifting in repose, the whisper of hawthorn blooms in the breeze, and below them all, the thud of Danu's staff and laughter like the purist of chimes.

About the Author

L.A. Alber is the author of three previous novels—*Kilmoon*, nominated for a Rosebud Award for best first novel; *Whispers in the Mist*; and *Path Into Darkness*, a finalist for the Spotted Owl Award. Winner of an Elizabeth George Foundation writing grant and a Walden Fellowship, and a Pushcart Prize nominee, you'll most often find her lounging in bistros with red wine, laptop, and a tiny terrier at her feet. She lives in Portland, Oregon.

www.lisaalber.com

The Original

DUNGEON SOLITAIRE

Tomb of Four Kings

Still Available for Free

at

matthewlowes.com/games

Complete Rules
are Print-Ready and Playable
with any Standard Deck
of Playing Cards

Dungeon Solitaire
Labyrinth of Souls

TAROT CARD GAME

by Matthew Lowes

Illustrated by Josephe Vandel

Complete Rulebook
&
Labyrinth of Souls Tarot Deck
Available at
matthewlowes.com/games

Labyrinth of Souls Fiction
Coming Soon
Mountain of Ashes by John Reed
Bayou's Lament by Cheryl Owen-Wilson
Perilous by Cynthia Coate-Ray

... and more to come!
information at
shadowspinnerspress.com

www.ingramcontent.com/pod-product-compliance
Lightning Source LLC
Chambersburg PA
CBHW021016120726
47905CB00009B/3041